Letter to My Mother

Texts and Translations

The MLA series Texts and Translations was founded in 1991 to provide students and faculty members with important texts and high-quality translations that otherwise would not be available at an affordable price. The books in the series are aimed at students in upper-level undergraduate and graduate courses—in national literatures in languages other than English, comparative literature, literature in translation, ethnic studies, area studies, and women's studies.

For a complete listing of titles, see the last pages of this book.

EDITH BRUCK

Letter to My Mother

Translated by Brenda Webster
with Gabriella Romani

Introduced by Gabriella Romani

The Modern Language Association of America
New York   2006

MLA and the MODERN LANGUAGE ASSOCIATION are trade-
marks owned by the Modern Language Association of America.
For information about obtaining permission to reprint material
from MLA book publications, send your request by mail (see address below) or e-mail (permissions@mla.org).

Library of Congress Cataloging-in-Publication Data

Bruck, Edith.
[Lettera alla madre. English]
Letter to my mother / Edith Bruck ; translated by Brenda Webster
with Gabriella Romani ; introduced by Gabriella Romani.
pages cm. — (Texts and translations ; 18)
Includes bibliographical references.
ISBN-13: 978-0-87352-936-5 (paperback ; alk. paper)
ISBN-10: 0-87352-936-7 (alk. paper)
1. Holocaust, Jewish (1939–1945)—Fiction. 2. Holocaust
survivors—Fiction. 3. Women—Italy—Fiction.
I. Webster, Brenda S. II. Romani, Gabriella. III. Title.
PQ4862.R7L4813 2006
853'.914—dc22   2006033181

Texts and Translations 18
ISSN 1079-2538
Second printing 2016

Cover illustration: *La madre*, by Marino Melarangelo.
Pastel on paper. 100 × 70 cm. Used by permission of the artist.

Printed on recycled paper

Published by The Modern Language Association of America
85 Broad Street, suite 500, New York, New York 10004-2434
www.mla.org

TABLE OF CONTENTS

Introduction
vii

Suggestions for Further Reading
xxiii

Works by Bruck
xxv

Translator's Note
xxvii

Letter to My Mother

Letter to My Mother
3

Traces
129

INTRODUCTION

Letter to My Mother: The Context

Written in 1988, more than forty years after the Holocaust, *Letter to My Mother* provides a testimony unique
among Auschwitz survivors, using memory to speak as
much to the present and the future as to the past. Edith
Bruck has devoted her entire adult life to bearing witness,
through both her literary works and public appearances,
to the atrocities she experienced in the Nazi concentration
camps. The author of more than ten volumes of prose
and several poetry collections, she has created a mosaic of
testimonial narratives that describe the survivor's search
for self-identity and meaning in the very act of testimony.
Her narrative responds to the urgency, often invoked
by survivors, to give voice to those who can no longer
speak, and at the same time it seeks to create a dialogue
between past and present, between her generation and
those to follow. In the face of recent events, such as the
genocide in Rwanda and the outbreak of ravaging wars
around the world; the resurgence of anti-Semitism; and
persistent bigotry and racism, Bruck's unrelenting voice
reminds us of one of the darkest moments in the history
of humankind and recalls its devastating consequences in

the lives of people and nations. In this context, testimony constitutes the painstaking effort to bring the past into the present and, to borrow Eli Wiesel's words, to turn "experience into knowledge" (1).

Born into a poor Jewish family on 3 May 1932, in Tiszabèrcel, a small Hungarian village situated along the river Tisza near the border with Ukraine and Slovakia, Edith Bruck (pseudonym of Edith Steinschreiber) was deported with her family to the concentration camps of Auschwitz, Dachau, Christianstadt, Landsberg, and Bergen-Belsen, where she lost both her parents and a brother. After the war she lived in Israel for three years, but, dissatisfied with her life in that country, she left in 1954. On her way to Argentina she stopped in Rome, where she decided to remain and where she has lived ever since. Soon after moving to Italy, she wrote her first book, *Chi ti ama così* (1959; *Who Loves You like This* [2001]), an autobiographical account of her life beginning with her childhood in Hungary. With the exception of three books, *Mio splendido disastro* (1979; "My Wonderful Disaster"), *Il silenzio degli amanti* (1997; "The Lovers' Silence"), and *L'amore offeso* (2002; "A Tormented Love")—narratives on the theme of love, the first and third drawing on her long-standing and tumultuous relationship with the poet Nelo Risi—all Bruck's works are devoted to her experience of the concentration camps, thus providing some of the most compelling testimony of the Holocaust in the Italian language.

From the very beginning of her literary career, with *Chi ti ama così* (based on a manuscript that the author began in 1945 but lost in her wanderings in Eastern Europe immediately after the war), Bruck adopted the Italian language—an "accidental choice," as she puts it—as her main linguistic tool for literary production (see McGlinn). Her books have since been translated into several languages, including her native Hungarian. The choice to use Italian instead of Hungarian was a conscious strategy, to create a certain detachment from the object of her descriptions and a narrative voice that would enable her to endure the emotional distress caused by painful memories. She explained in an interview:

> Just because [Italian] isn't mine, it permits me certain things that I couldn't do in my first language, the one in my blood, my veins, my culture. Between a writer and the maternal language there is a sort of shame, a brake that keeps you from saying certain things. The language that isn't yours removes that brake.   (Webster 174)

Bruck's Italian is peculiarly unadorned and concise. In syntax and lexicon, it is markedly different from the more ornate prose typically produced by Italian writers of her generation. The difference can be explained by the lack of an emotional "brake," mentioned by the author, which entailed the use of the Italian language as a basic, utilitarian mode of self-expression, as if she were an artisan in need of a tool. Also, she did not attend the Italian school system and was not exposed to lessons in traditional composition, which would certainly have shaped her Italian literary voice. Further, the directness and relative simplicity of her language may be the result of poetic and ideological considerations, which led the author to choose a linguistic medium that would reveal the most yet be unobtrusive. Like a pioneer, Bruck found in the land and language of her adopted Italy a fruitful terrain for her literary expression, and she developed a distinctive narrative voice based on her personal and cultural history and her determination to write. Her literary persona is the product of a forced displacement and cannot easily be defined in any one national and cultural set of traditions. She shares this status with other authors who adopted a language as their expressive medium—for example, Elie Wiesel and Ruth Klüger.

When Bruck moved to Rome in 1954, Italy was going through a process of great social and economic transformation. It was then still a largely peasant country made up of a few big cities and a multitude of rural provinces, each having a distinct cultural identity and a local dialect. In the immediate postwar period, after twenty years of Fascism with its economic policies of self-sufficiency and five years of devastating war (including two years of civil war), the country embarked on a new era, signaled by the constitutional change from monarchy to republic and animated by a spirit of moral rebirth and economic reconstruction. The cultural life of those years was also imbued with this enthusiasm. Intellectuals, many of whom had participated in the anti-Fascist resistance movement, reflected in their works the hopes and dreams of a generation of Italians who wanted to take part in this process of renewal. This generation longed for the sense of national unity that had inspired the Risorgimento movements, but despite the 1860 political unification, the country had failed to acquire a real modern national identity.

A notable example of postwar artistic commitment was cinematic neorealism, which began in 1945 and officially lasted about a decade. The phenomenon spilled over into other artistic fields, including literature. Born in reaction to the escapist cinema of the Fascist era and to such contemporary literary models as decadentism and poetic formalism—perceived as too elegiac and aloof—neorealism, although never constituting a formal artistic group, was led by such filmmakers as Vittorio De Sica, Cesare Zavattini, Roberto Rossellini, and Luchino Visconti and literati like Elio Vittorini, Cesare Pavese, and Vasco Pratolini. Whatever their differences, all subscribed to the principle that art must adhere as much as possible to the reality and authenticity of the experience represented. Modeled after the nineteenth-century literary movement of verismo, the Italian version of naturalism, neorealism strove to describe reality with scientific precision. The films produced according to this poetics (Rossellini's *Open City* and De Sica's *Bicycle Thief,* to cite two of the most famous) are characterized by a shared set of cinematic rules: use of location shooting, natural lighting, true-to-life subjects, working-class protagonists, and nonprofessional cast. As a meaningful cinematic practice, neorealism ended in 1952, but it remains to this day an inspiring force for the Italian film industry (Marcus 22–35).

During the 1950s, Rome was not only the geographic epicenter of neorealism, it was also the center around which the national cultural life gravitated (Asor Rosa and Cicchetti 642). Arriving there in 1954, Bruck soon found herself immersed in the intellectual life of the city as she became acquainted with writers such as Carlo Levi, Vittorini, Pratolini, Alberto Moravia, and Zavattini; with Zavattini she began a fruitful artistic collaboration.[1] While it would be hard if not impossible to pin down the specific linguistic or stylistic influences these writers had on Bruck's writing, since her literary language is very different from theirs, it is undeniable that her narrative voice emerged from a poetic and ideological environment related to the poetics of the neorealists, who shared with her the belief that reality ought to be an intrinsic element of narrative. The neorealists' commitment to an art engagé could only validate her claim for poetic recognition of a literature born out of a hard-learned lesson of real life. Once in Rome, she found in neorealism the same moral and artistic concerns that inspired her to write. While this is not to say that Bruck should be considered a neorealist writer, the movement certainly influenced, at both the ideological and poetic level, her determination to write her testimony in Italy.

Not all survivors managed or wished to publish their writings immediately after the war. It is well known, for instance, that Primo Levi's *If This Is a Man* was first rejected in 1947 by Natalia Ginzburg, then editor for Einaudi, a prominent leftist publisher, and that Levi had to resort to the smaller De Silva publishing house in Turin, which was able to sell only a few copies of what later became one of the most cited works of Holocaust literature. Other survivors, like Giuliana Tedeschi, decided to publish their memoirs only much later. In fact, Tedeschi's *C'è un puntino sulla terra: Una donna nel lager di Birkenau* (*There Is a Place on Earth: A Woman in Birkenau* [1992]), written

soon after the war, remained in a drawer for forty years
before reaching the reading public in 1988. The delay,
Tedeschi explained, resulted both from her reluctance to
expose her young daughters to the horrors of her imprisonment and from her impression that people during the
euphoric postwar reconstruction efforts were unwilling
to listen to past stories of pain and death (Padoan 165–
66). A similar delay may be found in the work of another
Italian writer of Holocaust literature, Liana Millu, who,
after publishing in 1947 a collection of short stories, *Il
fumo di Birkenau* (*Smoke over Birkenau* [1991]), which was
unfairly ignored by critics and readers alike, decided to
return to writing only much later in 1978, with *I ponti di
Schwerin* ("The Bridges of Schwerin") (Branciforte 296).

Edith Bruck's literary production does not seem to
have been similarly affected in the postwar period, because it spans over five decades. She is indeed the most
prolific writer of Holocaust narrative in the Italian language. In recognition of her work, she has received several literary prizes, among them the prestigious Premio
Rapallo and Premio Città di Penne for *Lettera alla madre*
(*Letter to My Mother*).

Bruck's *Letter to My Mother* has more recently been
also the focus of a traveling exhibit, composed of twenty-
three artworks produced by young Italian artists who
were asked to put into images their readings of the tor-
tuous path of World War II history and in particular of
the Holocaust. The show, titled *From Novel to Exhibit:
Twenty-Three Artists Meet Edith Bruck*, was organized by
the Hannah Arendt Cultural Association of Teramo, an
Italian city in the southern region of Abruzzo. It opened

on 4 December 2003 in Teramo, then moved to Pescara on 24 January for the celebration of the national Day of Memory. On 23 April 2004 it was shown at the Italian Cultural Institute in Budapest, where the author herself, along with the young artists and organizers, introduced the paintings and sculptures to the local authorities and public. The mobile nature of the exhibit is significant, as it embodies the aim of most testimonial literature, including Bruck's narrative: to foster awareness of the historical event by reaching out to as large an audience as possible, thus providing exchange among different generations, in which incomprehensible events can be made imaginatively accessible.

Letter to My Mother: The Text

Letter to my Mother represents a landmark in Bruck's writing, a bridge between her early and more recent work. In this text, for the first time she forthrightly engages experimental narrative techniques to address the question of self-identity in relation to testimony and, more specifically, to her reality as a woman who must reconcile her past and present life with an uncomfortably assumed public role as a survivor. The book centers on the theme of loss, of rupture caused by a traumatic event, and on the power of language to help recover part of one's past through the painstaking work of imaginative reconciliation. Though looking backward, the book's main focus is the present.

Published a year after Levi's suicide in 1987, *Letter to My Mother* may be read as a narrative response to the disappearance of her longtime friend and fellow writer, whom Bruck commonly referred to as an intellectual father figure. She knew Levi well; they met in the 1970s and saw each other frequently for personal and professional reasons. United by "the invisible thread," as she put it, "that exists among survivors" (48) and by both being writers of Holocaust literature, they developed a strong relationship of mutual respect. Levi's sudden death—described by the author in *Letter to My Mother* as a shock and betrayal ("what pain, what paralyzing stupor")—depicted once again the specter of parental loss, sparking the need to return to the memory of her biological parents and to an exploration of her identity in the context of such loss.

Letter to My Mother is a tribute to the parental figure and is composed of two parts: "Letter to My Mother," developed as an imaginary dialogue with her deceased mother, and "Traces," a fictional story based on the theme of a journey without return; a father, in his old age, fails to connect to the present, remaining thus forever encapsulated in his past. Like a diptych, the two sections can be read independently, but it is in the whole product that the author's objective is realized: the exploration of the theme of displacement not only from one's land of origin and mother tongue but also from the primal source of emotional foundation, the family. Both maternal and paternal figures had been a source of creative inspiration for her narrative of testimony, but in *Letter to My Mother* they appear for the first time as complementary elements, at both the thematic and structural level, coalescing into a single project of self-recognition and cultural memory.

In the first section of the book, the narrative spans the time from the days when the author was still a child in Hungary to her postwar life in Italy. It does not proceed chronologically but begins from the moment daughter and mother are separated on their arrival at Auschwitz in 1944 and maintains an almost erratic relation to events and times, as descriptions of the author's childhood in Hungary switch back and forth to those of her adult life in Italy. Developed as a dialogue in absentia with her mother, Bruck's "Letter to My Mother" is a story situated at the boundaries of different literary genres: memoir, testimony, epistolary fiction, and historical biography.

Why does the author address the letter to her mother and not to her father or both parents? In Bruck's first testimonial book, *Chi ti ama così*, both parents appear in the narrative (although the figure of the mother is more enhanced), but "Letter to My Mother" privileges the mother as the narrator's main interlocutor. Feminist and psychoanalytic theories of creativity tend to identify the place of the mother as a main source for linguistic expression (Hirsch 52). If seen through the lens of these theories, Bruck's mother functions as a liminal figure, a narrative and psychological filter that allows the author to access and represent her world of memories, to connect to her past through a matrilinear genealogy. Like Dante in Primo Levi's *If This Is a Man*, Bruck's mother constitutes a main referent in the process of self-definition and provides inspiration for artistic and linguistic creation. In *If This Is a Man*, when trying to hold on to his "humanity," Levi evokes Dante from his past as a reader of literature. Levi refers to what Sandra Gilbert defined as a "relationship of sonship" (Gilbert and Gubar 6). It is through the memory of his schooldays, of his cultural past, of his literary knowledge, that he strives to recapture an identity otherwise negated by the Nazi regime's ideology of annihilation.

"Letter to My Mother" follows a similar retroactive path, though by way of a maternal instead of paternal referent. The figure of the mother functions as both the source of creative inspiration and the unifying theme of the text. The apex of this process of self-definition through the representation of the mother-daughter relationship is reached in the final scene when the narrator recites the Kaddish (a prayer recited by men in Jewish tradition) and asks her mother to let herself be soothed as if her mother were the daughter. By inverting the roles and blurring the differences between mother and daughter, Bruck invokes a state of fusion with the maternal body and their common past. When, during a conversation in 1996, I asked Bruck why she created an imaginative dialogue with her mother and not with both parents, she stated that she could remember only her mother's voice. Her father was always very quiet at home, a silent and absent figure for her even before their forced separation.[2] Her mother was the parent to whom she turned for both physical and spiritual nurturing.

More broadly, Bruck's focus on the mother-daughter relationship relates to her interest in gender issues, to her search for artistically viable strategies that reflect her identity as a woman and as a Holocaust survivor. Her interest in themes related to the construction of a female subjectivity may be traced to the feminist debates of the

1970s and 1980s and to the shift of emphasis from a purely material and economic analysis of women's oppression to a more philosophical and psychological approach to the question of women's liberation. This approach emphasized the exploration of the female unconscious, as in the practice of *autocoscienza* ("consciousness raising"), and the construction of a female epistemology outside the patriarchal order (Lazzaro-Weiss 33–47). "Letter to My Mother" portrays the Holocaust from a female perspective, highlighting the role of gender in the creation of memory. As Bruck has said:

> Certainly Italian mothers and daughters have recognized themselves in my description of dependency—of hate and love. Many mothers have recognized themselves in this mother and many daughters in the daughter. Many readers have written to me saying, "My mother is the same.". . . So I would not say it was specifically about the relations between a mother dead at Auschwitz and a daughter who survived. It is something that could happen today. There are many daughters who can't make themselves understood. The mother can't see that the daughter is a separate person.   (Webster 172–73)

While Bruck's personal encounter with the Holocaust surely motivates her decision to write "Letter to My Mother," her experimental and fragmentary account of the mother-daughter relationship seeks, ultimately, to inscribe her personal story in a larger context of universal values, which are supposed to create empathy among human beings willing to listen and thus share the burden of memory (Laub 57). Indeed, even at the structural level,

"Letter to My Mother," with its epistolary format, facilitates the creation of a correspondence between writer and reader, who are thus united by a sort of epistolary pact. The readers of a letter, in fact, by virtue of their role as addressees, are compelled to participate in the creation of narrative meaning and respond, whether emotionally or intellectually, to the call of awareness and moral responsibility petitioned by the author (Altman 89).

The second part of *Letter to My Mother*, "Traces," recounts the author's decision, and eventual failure, to retrace her past by physically returning to Germany and reconnecting with the life she left in the concentration camps. She visits Dachau, where her father died, but forgets to pay tribute to him. Only on her return does she realize that, in her panic to leave the camps as soon as possible, she failed to remember him. Back in Italy, she decides to complete the writing of a story, started before her journey, about a Hungarian man, a survivor of Auschwitz, who moved to the United States and in his old age no longer speaks English and cannot recognize his family members. Even after his daughter takes him back to Hungary, he does not relate to his present life and remains forever trapped in a past that has permanently marked him.

The figure of the father, though fictional and imaginative (Bruck's father did not survive the Holocaust), is infused with strong autobiographical elements—based on two main characteristics ascribed by the author to her father: silence and marginality. The story within the story of this second section of the book exemplifies the difficult process of remembering and representing a trauma of the past. It further points to the solitude of the survivor who is left alone to carry the burden of memory against a pervasive and collective disposition to forget.

The theme of a journey appears throughout Bruck's work. Starting with *Chi ti ama così*, the author tells of her sense of loss after the war, recounting her wanderings first in Eastern Europe, then in Israel, a country that she depicts as far different from the promised land she knew through her mother's words. *Due stanze vuote* ("Two Empty Rooms") comprises three travel narratives, set respectively in Hungary, America, and Israel, all of which portray a story of disillusionment and ultimate failure to reconnect to the past. Judith, for instance, returns to her village in Hungary only to realize that time and events have thwarted any possible reconciliation with the villagers, who, now as before her deportation, perceive her as fundamentally different from them. *Transit* focuses on the difficulties that a survivor, who works as a consultant for a Holocaust film director, encounters when dealing face-to-face with her past. Linda, the protagonist, prematurely terminates her contract and her trip to Eastern Europe, where the film is being shot, frustrated because she had hoped to come to terms with her past but cannot and is aware of the danger of turning testimony into a complacently detached commodity.[3]

In *Letter to My Mother*, the theme of a journey is developed in a circular narrative frame, whereby the story begins and ends with the familiar environment of the household, from which the author is willing to separate only by way of storytelling. Written more than twenty-five years ago, the book provides a significant meditation on the complex task of representing the Holocaust. Although conscious that language constrains the representation of trauma, Bruck affirms that, through literature, history and imagination can meet in fruitful and unexpected ways.

Notes

I thank Pietro Frassica for introducing me to Edith Bruck's oeuvre many years ago, during a graduate course he offered as visiting professor at the University of Pennsylvania. Our discussions on Bruck's narrative of testimony have stayed with me and my scholarly work ever since.

1. Bruck cowrote with Zavattini the screenplay for the film *Andremo in città* (1966), directed by Nelo Risi and based on Bruck's novel of the same title. Geraldine Chaplin and Nino Castelnuovo starred in the film.

2. The father in "Letter to My Mother" is portrayed as a victim, a poor man marginalized both in society, because of his social, economic, and ethnic identity, and in his family, for whom he cannot provide the basic necessities of life.

3. Bruck's narrative of return to Hungary anticipates the journey that she actually made in 1983 and that became a film, titled *The Visit*, produced by Hungarian Public Television and directed by Lazlo Rèvèsz.

Works Cited

Altman, Janet Gurkin. *Epistolarity: Approaches to a Form*. Columbus: Ohio State UP, 1982.

Asor Rosa, Alberto, and Angelo Cicchetti. "Roma." *Letteratura italiana*. Vol. 3. Turin: Einaudi, 1987. 547–652.

Branciforte, Susanna. "Intervista con la storia: Una conversazione con Liana Millu." *Italianist* 18 (1998): 288–304.

Bruck, Edith. "L'amico, il parente, il fratello." *Primo Levi: Il presente del passato: Giornate internazionali di studio.* Ed. Alberto Cavaglion. Milan: FrancoAngeli, 1991. 48–51.

Gilbert, Sandra, and Susan Gubar. *The Madwoman in the Attic: The Woman Writer and the Nineteenth-Century Literary Imagination.* New Haven: Yale UP, 1979.

Hirsch, Marianne. *The Mother/Daughter Plot: Narrative, Psychoanalysis, Feminism.* Bloomington: Indiana UP, 1989.

Laub, Dori. "Bearing Witness; or, The Vicissitudes of Listening." *Testimony: Crises of Witnessing in Literature, Psychoanalysis, and History.* By Shoshana Felman and Laub. New York: Routledge, 1992. 57–74.

Lazzaro-Weiss, Carole. *From Margins to Mainstream: Feminism and Fictional Modes in Italian Women's Writing, 1968–1990.* Philadelphia: U of Pennsylvania P, 1993.

Levi, Primo. *If This Is a Man: Remembering Auschwitz.* New York: Summit, 1986.

Marcus, Millicent. *Italian Film in the Light of Neorealism.* Princeton: Princeton UP, 1986.

McGlinn, Marguerite. *An Interview with Edith Bruck, Author of Who Loves You like This.* 4 Oct. 2005 <http://www.pauldrybooks.com/complete_catalog/wholovesyou/An%20Interview%20with%20Edith%20Bruck.htm>.

Padoan, Daniela. *Come una rana d'inverno.* Milan: Bompiani, 2004.

Webster, Brenda. "An Interview with Edith Bruck." *Thirteenth Moon* 11.1–2 (1993): 170–75.

Wiesel, Elie. "Art and the Holocaust." *New York Times* 11 June 1989: 1+.

SUGGESTIONS FOR FURTHER READING

Ciccarelli, Andrea. "Frontier, Exile, and Migration in the Contemporary Italian Novel." *The Cambridge Companion to the Italian Novel.* Ed. Peter Bondanella and Ciccarelli. Cambridge: Cambridge UP, 2003. 197–213.

Di Sabatino, Guendalina, ed. Lettera alla madre: *Dal romanzo alla mostra itinerante: 23 artisti incontrano Edith Bruck.* Teramo: Centro di Cultura delle Donne Hannah Arendt, 2004.

Giorgio, Adalgisa. "Dall'autobiografia al romanzo: La rappresentazione della Shoa nell'opera di Edith Bruck." *Le donne delle minoranze: Le ebree e protestanti d'Italia.* Ed. Claire E. Honess and Verina R. Jones. Turin: Claudiana, 1999.

———. "Strategies for Remembering: Auschwitz, Mother, and Writing in Edith Bruck." *European Memories of the Second World War.* Ed. Helmut Peitsch, Charles Burdett, and Claire Gorrara. New York: Berghahn, 1999. 247–55.

Levi, Primo. *If This Is a Man: Remembering Auschwitz.* New York: Summit, 1986.

Millu, Liana. *Smoke over Birkenau.* Trans. Lynne Sharon Schwartz. Philadelphia: Jewish Pub. Soc., 1991.

Tedeschi, Giuliana. *There Is a Place on Earth: A Woman in Birkenau.* Trans. Tim Parks. New York: Pantheon, 1992.

Wilson, Rita. "Contradictory Cultures: Edith Bruck and Giuliana Morandini." *Speculative Identities, Contemporary Italian Women's Narratives.* Leeds: Northern UP, 2000. 99–111.

WORKS BY BRUCK

1959. *Chi ti ama così*. Trans. as *Who Loves You like This*. Trans. Thomas Kelso. Philadelphia: Dry, 2001.

1962. *Andremo in città*

1969. *Le sacre nozze*

1974. *Due stanze vuote*

1975. *Il tatuaggio*

1978. *Transit*

1979. *Mio splendido disastro*

1980. *In difesa del padre*

1988. *Lettera alla madre*

1990. *Monologo*

1993. *Nuda proprietà*

1995. *L'attrice*

1997. *Il silenzio degli amanti*

1998. *Itinerario: Poesie scelte*

1999. *Signora Auschwitz: Il dono della parola*

2002. *L'amore offeso*

2004. *Lettera da Francoforte*

2005. *Specchi*

TRANSLATOR'S NOTE

My translation of *Lettera alla madre* is the result of a fruitful collaboration with Gabriella Romani. As is well known, many translators work in tandem with a native speaker. While I could use my sensibility and years of work as a novelist to craft a style in English for Bruck's powerful, sometimes tormented evocation of her experience in the camps, Gabriella was able to provide deeper insights into the subtleties of the Italian. I started with a literal translation to make sure I had grasped Bruck's inner intentions, sometimes consulting Bruck herself as I worked my way toward a vital rendition of the text. Throughout this process Gabriella was exceedingly helpful, reading and commenting in detail on each draft. The task of finding the right tone, always a critical issue for translators, was made more difficult by the fact that Bruck is writing of feelings and experiences almost beyond language. As one of her reviewers aptly put it, "you can no more criticize this book than you could the Bible" (Portinari). It is a work of testimony, and I felt it deserved the strongest and at the same time the sparest translation to bring out its eloquence.

BW

Work Cited

Portinari, Folco. "Memoria di Auschwitz." *L'unità* 3 Aug. 1988: 13.

EDITH BRUCK

Letter to My Mother

LETTER TO MY MOTHER

How many times I've started to write you! A hundred, a thousand? I don't know. I only know I wrote and threw away the pages one after another, the way you do when you begin a letter to someone you deeply love and aren't sure you're loved back.

I don't even have a clear idea of what I'm going to say to you, it's a mystery even to me. It's something that leaves neither of us in peace. What's certain, the only thing that's certain, is that there is something suspended between us, maybe only infinite silence or a distance that can't be bridged. The brief time we had together is an indissoluble bond but also painfully, often unbearably, extraneous. Maybe your faith is to blame, you had enough to spare, and I don't have enough even for myself. By faith I mean belief in God, in a real God. Belief in hell, in heaven, in divine justice. I feel uneasy even listing the requirements for belief. I lack imagination in the realm of faith. I haven't even read the Bible through to the end, the only reading we could have had in common, your only source of culture, learned by heart from time immemorial.

I warn you that I'm going to write everything that comes to mind, I'll say it all, I won't hide anything from you. How could I? I need you precisely in order not to lie or betray but to be myself, even if it pleases neither one of us. We didn't choose each other, we're mother and daughter by chance, and since you were my mother I loved you and will always love you the way they do in fairy tales.

You conceived me by God's will as you did your other children. You didn't make love for love, though you loved my father, but out of duty. We were born by divine choice, as if we were God's children, not the children of you and Papa. Papa didn't seem to have anything to do with it, as if God himself had made you pregnant.

If it's true that the dead don't die, that they know everything, you'll know that I've lived in Rome for a lifetime. The second? The third? Let's say a leftover life, you know what I mean, don't you? So far you follow me and I hope you'll recognize yourself. Do you recognize me as your daughter, still resisting prayer?

No no, don't get mad now, don't go, listen to me! You have to. I'd better take your hand. That way you won't escape. You won't get away from me. This time you have to listen. You can't shut me up. Shake me off easily with

4

the excuse that you have work to do: patching our rags, washing, ironing, cleaning, fixing meals for your ever hungry children. You can't say anything if I don't let you speak. I'll be more generous than you were, I promise you. I'll let you say what I already know, I'll make you repeat what I've heard you say down to the last word, the very last word you said, your last testament: "Obey! obey!" You shouted letting my hand go, letting me go, pushing me away from you, letting the soldier's blows drive me to the other side, in the opposite direction.

Neither of us knew that you were going to the gas chambers and I to forced labor, toward a probable survival that happened who knows how or why.

"By God's will" you have your answer ready, but I won't let you say it because I don't want to fight with you now. I want peace! I have wanted it since the twenty-eighth of May, 1944. I still remember it as if it were today, a day that goes on forever, timeless, enclosing all time. I was menstruating. It was the fourth day of my period, Mama, the fourth day of our only trip together.

"This was all we needed," you said as they loaded us onto the wagon where there wasn't even a piece of paper to catch the blood that was running down my bare legs freezing at the end of May as if it were still January.

You tore a strip of your undergarment, just as Papa had torn his collar as a sign of mourning.

5

I already knew, you told me, that monthly bleeding meant I was a woman, I could have children when I married.

"Obey!!" you pushed me away while I fought wildly, screaming like a Christmas pig under its owner's knife. Because of me the soldier hit you, beat you. Forgive me, but how could I leave you, let myself be taken from you?

The blow you got hurt me more than all the blows I was getting myself. In fact I didn't even feel them anymore, but seeing you on the ground with your head in your hands hurt me so much that I obeyed instantly; running away, I came upon Golda, your favorite daughter; we embraced, we managed to stay together, living for each other, not dying for each other, even if Golda says I owe my life to her. Maybe so . . .

At the beginning of my imprisonment I cried so much, Mama, I called for you day and night, then I stopped. There was no place for anyone outside me, outside my life and Golda's. It was enough that we stayed alive. The death of others meant I was alive. I was breathing. I felt myself walking as I dragged the heaps of corpses meant for fertilizer toward the common ditch.

I didn't even look at the faces of the dead, I didn't listen to anyone who had breath left for a last word, I turned my back, what good would it have done to listen to them, to close their crazed eyes, to remove a few fleas, to pray?

To say a Shema, a final blessing over them, seemed the most absurd thing I could have done.

Should I be ashamed? Are you going to reproach me? Do you still dare reproach me? "I'm not ashamed," I answer you. And add that I was fortunate to have this job, the dead were feathers compared to the stones and beams we had to carry. They didn't weigh anything. They were all dislocated bones and eyes dead of hunger. I only did what I had to do, just like those who caused their death. Nothing more. Never a secret prayer or a human tear. I followed orders scrupulously, took no risks. The fear of death had absorbed all my energy, all my will and capacity to think.

I was dominated by fear and hunger, I didn't feel anything else. I don't know exactly when I changed so completely, becoming docile and obedient, maybe at the first pangs of hunger or the first corpse beside me. Between one day and the next I stopped being myself and I no longer cried for my mother. I was only one of the many prisoners terrorized by the Germans, by Mengele, by the Kapos, by whoever wasn't a simple prisoner like me. I thought about them constantly. At night I dreamed about them, during the day I spied on them, I hid myself from their sight. If you had prepared me for my future, Mama, instead of hiding the big secret, maybe I would have kept a little space for you in my heart. If nothing else, I would have remembered that you'd said this or that, that you'd foreseen, you who always knew everything, surely you must have known.

You could have said: "Listen children, you are risking your lives here, who knows where our Czech or Polish relatives have ended up. Let the adults decide for themselves, the children should hide if there is anyone who will hide them. We're old. We put ourselves in God's hands. He can't forget us. Whatever happens must happen, it is God's will."

Maybe it was better not to say anything, it would have happened just the same. We wouldn't have left you, your son Edy got false identity papers made in the city so he could join us in the ghetto and go to the death camps with us. Being together was the most important thing. The rest hardly mattered. The family was united. Dying together would be easier.

But if you had said, "You decide," one of us, even the youngest, might have taken a stick, a stone, or an ax and struck out before dying.

"If your mother agrees, I'll hide you," our neighbor, Mrs. Mari, proposed to me, but I didn't even mention it to you, I was afraid you might say yes and leave me there in the cellar with rats, and I'd never see you again.

"Did you tell your mother?" Mrs. Mari asked me several times.

"Yes, yes, yes," I lied without looking at her, talking in a low voice, telling her that Mama thanked her but she wasn't going to leave me alone.

"Ah, I knew it," she said to herself, "a mother loves her children. It's better this way. I don't put myself in danger and you're happy, eh?"

"Yes, my Mama told me we can't possibly separate," I thought to say, "I'm going with Mama."

"Where?" asked Mrs. Mari, but I didn't listen anymore, I ran home to you, clinging to your dress.

"What is it? What's the matter with you?" you asked, rejecting my impulsive love, as anxious as if you, not I, had to hide in that cellar.

The fear of losing you had become my only nightmare. I never felt fear for myself, my feelings were still healthy, only after a while did I stop feeling anything for anyone. As if only Golda and I still existed. The world consisted of the two of us. Of our bodies. Getting distracted from one's own life meant risking it. It was necessary to watch over it twenty-four hours a day. If the statistics are true, the average life expectancy at Auschwitz was two to three months. Whoever wanted to last longer, like me, had to become master of her life. Paradoxically our existence didn't depend on the murderers around us, it was up to us to walk or not walk when others stopped, to work even when others collapsed, to delouse ourselves when others let themselves be eaten by lice.

What fear of death and what irrational love of life. Why is existence precious in any circumstances and at any price?

How did we manage to become enemies so soon, even among ourselves and breathe a sigh of relief when someone else was chosen for the gas? And feel pleased when others made mistakes, even leading them along, pushing them to make mistakes so we wouldn't. Happy if a soldier drew us aside to wash his mess tin so we could lick it in secret.

Our only hope was to find something to eat in the garbage, a mouthful that wasn't too small or too rotten. That's how we lived, Mama, like ferocious beasts, not by thinking of our mother! I stopped asking myself if you were alive or dead. I felt nothing but hunger. I only wanted to eat. The days grew longer every day, every night seemed the last. Time stopped between a murky past and an equally murky future.

Only nature, seasons marked the course of the months with the infrequent sun of those regions, rain that was never kind, dirty snow, hostile ice. But I believe that we never live in real time, Mama, everything depends on the circumstances. On how we are. Where we are. And with whom. Anyway, and I'd almost say fortunately, you were quickly rid of any feeling, even if one day at Auschwitz is an eternity.

Because you still had a little bit of fat on you, they'd condemned you at a glance to become some kind of soap!

They didn't know how you moved when you were working, how strong you were, how hard you worked; you were worth more than all your daughters put together, including Golda, the good one.

Who knows if you would have survived with us? With me and Golda. Who knows how I might have continued to disappoint you with my childish egoism, my desire to survive at any cost. Golda would have thought about you, only you, and maybe she would have let me die. Your life would have been more important than mine. For me too. Maybe I would have given my life for yours. We lived because you weren't with us, like other holy mothers at Auschwitz. Seeing a mother die in the Lager made everyone mourn, seeing them live roused a moment of respect, we remembered that we were daughters, that we were born human.

I'm really happy that you weren't with us, Mama; seeing you dying day after day would have destroyed me.

You remember? Even when I was home, I couldn't stand your headaches, a toothache, a pain in the cheek, even a sigh hurt me, not to speak of your tears.

Who knows how many prayers you would have murmured night and day, how many sermons you would have preached making us die in a frenzy of prayer instead of turning our eyes to some potato peel or turnip we might steal.

With you we would have died a thousand times, it would have been enough for us to say a Shema and we'd have gone to the other world. You might even have bawled for a candle on Friday night, some of the mothers did, Mama, and it was as tragically painful as a madwoman crying for the moon.

If you had died with us like other mothers, who knows, we might have hidden your body like other daughters, so we could have your ration of broth. We might have stripped you the way they did, for your rags, to cover ourselves better so we wouldn't die of cold. Afterward we might have sold your spoon to someone who'd had hers stolen and who, though dying of hunger, offered her portion of bread to escape punishment.

Who knows, we might have become like stepdaughters and you egotistical like so many other mothers, reversing the roles.

How could I have mothered you? Golda could, she was a born mother, mine too.

And like a mother she offered herself to Mengele in my place. Would you have done it?

"I'll kill myself," Golda told me with a glance when Mengele's icy glance rejected her and pushed me into the group of those who'd been selected.

Neither of us wanted to live without the other. Our bond had never been so strong, we'd never loved each other so much. If Golda hadn't been waiting for me in the barracks at number 11, I would never have had the strength to escape from number 8 at dawn after a night of falsehoods from a mother like you, adept at consoling us and telling us lie after lie. She too, the whore, knew what our fate would be under Mengele's knife.

"I don't believe you," I told her, "go away. Don't tell me to be good. Don't touch me"—she wanted to caress me—"go away, I know very well where they're taking us."

"Don't shout," the slut ordered. She didn't want the others, already quieted by her reassurances, to hear me. She too followed orders. Everyone followed orders. She did everything she could to shut me up. Allowing the Germans to carry out their plans with the minimum disturbance, without screams, cries, useless rebellion.

A chain of lies, silences, secrets, complicity—ours too—was what permitted everything that happened.

Mama, why didn't that woman tell me: "Go! Escape! Try it. It's dark at dawn, there's so much confusion. They won't count you again." Why did I have to think of it myself? Why did she keep lying? To make the massacre easy for the murderers? Because she was afraid, for herself?

You see, even grown-ups feared for themselves, it wasn't just me. I already knew that any change would be dangerous. The most important thing was to avoid selection, to avoid being seen, not to exist if possible. And to obey everyone with bent head.

I confess that sometimes I was tempted to grab the gun from an armed guard after mealtimes and "Baam,

baam" to blast away to the last bullet. I missed my one chance to kill. If I didn't manage to do it there . . . Should I have done it? Should I?

I'm not saying I would have been glad to die, Mama, in fact, since I didn't want to die, the thought of killing immediately passed. But at least if I'd been able to hit the uniformed adolescent who always spit at me and laughed in my face, I wouldn't be alive today, but I'd have died with a unique satisfaction. That boy gave me a new sensation, a homicidal hatred, maybe because he was near my age, and only at that age is it possible to enjoy a sense of power beyond punishment. Free. Insatiable.

He must have spit on me a thousand times collecting his poisonous saliva and taking aim at my bare limbs one after another as I was waiting to be deloused.

Though I hate violence, I still ask myself why I didn't have the courage to react, to become a human being, why I didn't redeem my dignity.

I'm not sure if I'm sorry that I put up with so much, that I spent a whole year being careful not to get out of line or break the Nazi rule, which would have brought instant death—certainly not Almighty God, Mama!

If I had obeyed you I would have been the most servile daughter in the world. I would have been a poor idiot. I wouldn't have done anything but try to figure out what you wanted, observe your steps, your looks, in order to serve you, and to defend myself at opportune moments.

I was an almost exemplary prisoner, and I learned everything quickly the way I did at school.

Even the guard at times couldn't resist my humility, my age, or my way of begging with my eyes and would throw me an extra potato, a leftover, an apple peel (not even he wallowed in food). And I thanked him with bent head, bowing with a woman's smile, an ass kisser's grin, anything so as not to die. How disgusting, Mama!

Never a true rebellion that would make it clear they were murderers, criminals. I didn't want to offend them even with a glance, never a sane, normal human reaction. Never a false step or a risk. Not even an extra word for the Jewish Kapos who had learned the lesson right away. Mengele's attention lingered on me only once, not through my own fault but because of someone else who had been selected and who had run against the electric fence.

She did well, better a single shock than to be cut in pieces with your eyes open, conscious.

"You," the doctor pointed his finger at me, I don't know why I remember him with white gloves and a conductor's baton in his hand. "Me, me!" Golda offered, like the heroine she was. If I hadn't escaped and come back at dawn, she would have committed suicide. It was like an unspoken pact between us, to stay together or die.

Staying alert even among the other prisoners was the most exhausting thing. At first, this was a painful surprise, later there was no feeling.

"Piece of shit, disgusting dammed Jewish whore," screamed Golda when a newly deported prisoner (like us) first slapped me. A girl from a nearby village. The daughter of Schuster, the shoemaker, adept at stealing the little bits of carrot and potato from the bottom of the broth she distributed.

A slap because I wasn't holding the mess tin straight for her to ladle its meager portion of soup, another slap because I dared to ask for more.

"You'll die too. God will punish you. You won't dare go home because if you do, I'll strangle you with my bare hands," thundered Golda, defending me and shielding herself from the blows that rained on us both. Then we cried holding each other, afraid because there was no more hope, even among ourselves.

Sometimes we still showed signs of shame when we fought and hurt each other in front of the enemy who laughed, pleased that we were destroying ourselves unaided.

Not me, Mama, don't worry, I never raised my hand against a fellow inmate, I never stole even a bit of bread guarded with sick jealousy, I never pushed anyone into serious danger. I never denounced anyone who robbed me, perhaps involuntarily someone died in my place, but that's usual in extreme circumstances.

And I owe my, our, behavior to the morality you transmitted to us with our blood. With your commandments. Maybe I really owe to you the inexplicable force that suddenly awoke in me when I swore I couldn't take another step. It was over, but I was still walking, I began to live all over again, I worked, I breathed, you gave birth to me again with your breath. How many times? I don't know. It seemed to me that the strength was mine, that it depended entirely on me and you weren't involved at all, I didn't even think of you! Was that true?

"You won't know how to take care of your own children," you sighed.

I don't have children, you know, but not because of your fears. Today I believe and console myself by saying that it's better this way, I would have been too much of a mother, I would have loved my children too much, been too afraid for them. Like Golda, I would have given them everything, I would have lived for them. I would have told them too much about the camps or too little. Told them too late or too soon. Being a survivor and a parent isn't easy, and it isn't easy to be a child marked by a parent's experience.

Even Edy, Mama, fears for his only son. The children of certain parents leave early. Almost as though they blame their parents for their past, their inescapable heredity.

17

I don't know when or how I would have told my children about the camps. And what would they have understood? Who can ever understand Auschwitz? And how could I have explained it to make it believable, real, it's more absurd and irrational than Hiroshima. There is no suitable time to tell about Auschwitz.

I would have made a mistake with my children, the way Golda did with her daughter who bears your name, Sara. Golda told her about Auschwitz while she held her to her breast, the baby sucked with blood and tears because the young mother had small nipples and tears that flowed too easily.

What should a reasonable parent do? Withhold everything, the way you did with us, or dispense the poison drop by drop?

It's a blessing not to have to tell my children anything. Maybe this is why I didn't have any. Not to have to spare them, biting my tongue the way you did, trusting everything to God.

While Europe burned and we with it, and America closed its doors, you waited for a miracle, you believed in miracles, like the Christians. "A miracle will happen," you said every day, scanning the sky.

I almost scanned it too. Later I asked myself what my mother expected from a sky empty of everything but clouds, rain, ice, hail, sun, stars, the moon!

Sometimes it made me laugh, forgive me, it hurt me too, I felt that you were so naive, you didn't understand anything.

"Lucky you," you told me. "Lucky you," I wanted to say, but I didn't dare. In those days parents were sacred and children ungrateful and barely respected in relation to God, who gave them life.

Poor Mama, you thought that I, your youngest, hadn't understood anything. But I did, much more than I was allowed. If I hadn't understood more, more than anyone, including you, I wouldn't be writing to you now. And maybe it would have been better for both of us. You would have had a happier daughter and I would have left you in peace, would have spared you reading this. Maybe up there in the world beyond, you don't even have a decent pair of glasses.

I know I do nothing but doubt, but I can't imagine you as a wealthy woman, compensated for everything, even the loss of your children. If justice were done, you should have everything you want, you should even have servants to massage your tired feet and swollen ankles—your head that was always hurting.

If only you were really up there surrounded by angels ready to satisfy all your desires, but I'm afraid the fable ends with life. If I've learned my lesson well, if I've lived my life well, there is nothing to regret.

I don't say one should die young—though I don't envy young people—you must do anything you can, especially to get out of Auschwitz, out of Mengele's hands; this is the real miracle, Mama! To die of old age in a white bed is ordinary, it's human, Mama, it can even be beautiful. My mother-in-law had a good death. She had an unearthly beauty, and if she hadn't been so terribly cold, I would have said she was setting off toward a new life.

Never was a dead person so cold; maybe because I never kissed a corpse. On the contrary, I used to push them away as if they had caught death and might infect me.

Of all the dead bodies I had seen and touched, I only felt such great cold with one. One can have more effect than a multitude.

When I kissed her, it was as though my mouth were flooded with a cold so deep, it could only have come from an endless death.

"What do you know about it?" you say in a soft voice—too soft—but that's all you say. You don't reveal the mystery. The great secrets of life and death you keep to yourself, while I'm still wondering every day how you ever managed to believe in a miracle.

Who could believe that a life this brutal, whose only advances are technological, would be judged in some hereafter—that our short life is only a rehearsal for some grand finale, a mirror for God? But who, if not He, the only God we have, is responsible for everything, good and evil? And if He is responsible, then no one is guilty.

If you kept your faith to the end, Mama, then dying was nothing—a liberation, the long-awaited passage to the real life. Perhaps you had just time for a moment of outrage at the way you reached your long-awaited destination. Who knows what you thought besides your hasty prayer before the gas took your last breath. Oh how I would love to know. How I wish you'd tell me that I'm wrong and you have always been right. That it was my mistake not to believe in God's magic wand, which if it existed would make him a sort of Mengele of the Heavens.

I am hurting you, I know, it hurts me too, to say these things. I wish I could believe that you are alive, waiting to give me all the good things I never received from you, things you could never give me—to make me the daughter of the richest woman instead of the daughter of the poorest mother. Mama, it is beautiful to imagine the unimaginable. I wish it were true for you—not for me. What hurts me is your life and your death.

If you had survived, I would really have made it up to you. I would have done anything for you. In secret, I would even have been a whore or a thief so that you wouldn't lack for anything.

Golda and Edy with their packed refrigerator would have given you all the material things: flannel for your dresses, shoes specially made for your deformed feet, ko-sher meat, plenty of candles for Friday nights, new head scarves for all the ceremonies.

I wouldn't force you to eat the same things I eat—you, who wouldn't let me touch pork even if I were starving.

Maybe I eat everything now to defy you. Maybe it's you I'm rebelling against. Weren't you God for me? Except without His opaque side. I know if you'd survived you wouldn't have asked for much. You'd have lived with Golda or Edy, not with me. They still pray—maybe a lit-tle less—but they wouldn't dare stop praying. They think I'm silent in temple because I can't pray in Hebrew. They can't even imagine that I have doubts. For them, believ-ing in God is as natural as eating or drinking, nothing complicated about it. God simply exists and has the last word. Golda has some grudges against God. Sometimes she tells me, speaking softly so He won't hear her, that there are moments when she doubts His existence. Then she becomes frightened of her own thoughts and adds, "But He must exist. He can't possibly not exist."

Golda is very nice, Mama, but she's also hard, difficult, a bit infantile. She gets angry easily, and anyone is in trou-ble who gets in the way of her angry look or her harsh tongue, swollen as a mother's heart, no longer sisterly.

Age isn't bringing us closer, it's pushing us apart—life does the rest. Her children are everything to her, she lives for them. She always lives for others. She has never learned to live for herself. She won't allow herself to be happy. This is her way of feeling close to you. She says she is the one who is most like you and that she loved you most.

You'd prefer me to be like her, wouldn't you? A good Jew. Faithful wife. Exemplary mother. Ideal grandmother. Amen. But is she happy? Would you ever have asked her? I would. And I know that she isn't happy. And I'm sorry. Terribly.

Maybe what's right for you is wrong for me. Would we have kept on taking opposite sides? How infuriating! You're my mother. Is it possible I'm understood better by a stranger? Even a Catholic?

"No one understands you," you said with delighted irony, half a century ago. "Poor thing. Go away, go on. You don't know what you are saying. Nothing you do is blessed."

When you talked like this, though I was happy to get out of washing the dishes, I felt bad inside and would snap back. "Let Golda help you, she is the clever one. I don't know how to do anything. Together you two are the world's greatest." I would provoke you, being careful that your hands couldn't reach me, that they'd stay where they were in the basin, on the iron, among dirty clothes or the feathers being plucked from a slaughtered kosher duck. I was less afraid of you and Golda together than I was when one of you decided to pick on me. The youngest are always at the mercy of their elders, just as the weak are of the strong, the less of the more powerful. It's the same inside and outside the family. Family and society reflect each other.

I'd be in serious trouble if I dared to raise my voice to you, Mama. Only you were allowed to raise yours to everyone. Actually, like all Jews, you and Papa were relatively civilized parents compared to the Protestant or Catholic peasants who beat their children like slaves, blinding or crippling them or breaking their heads. They did what they wanted with their children—no one would defend the children—they were part of their estate, needed for work. A small child could cry all day at the edge of a field, maybe even tied to a tree—only the midday bell had a voice, only the sun, rising or setting, marked time. A lunatic could scream his head off before someone peeked through the door of the cellar where he was chained forever.

The world of the peasants wasn't a good one. It was hard even to itself. Brutalized by work. Deaf and thick-witted, the peasants vented their impotent rage on their children, their animals, and each other.

The Jew was the opposite of the peasant—perhaps that was why there wasn't much love for us—we were the best of the worst. There was nothing we didn't put up with, and we kept trying to learn. I had to take Hebrew lessons even if going to class was torture. Wasn't that violence?

"No, no, no I won't go!" I screamed. "He's mean. He hurts me. He hits me with his stick. He spits on me when he talks. He hates me, Mama! I don't want to go!"

"That holy man!" you said indignantly. "If it weren't for him you wouldn't know Hebrew. He gives you lessons to please God. He has thirteen children, that hole of a shop with nothing in it except his poor wife waiting for someone to come in. It's only the Holy Spirit that keeps them alive."

"Why doesn't he work in the shop?" I protested. "He doesn't do anything."

You looked at me as though I were a worm. "Nothing? He studies, prays, he's not a pagan like your father. Thank God he's teaching you something."

So much good faith, Mama, with what tenderness I remember your words. Do you remember them? I bet you don't. If the dead remembered, what sort of dead would they be? What freedom would one get by dying? Would their remembering make the world any better? It doesn't make sense, Mama.

"Didn't you hear Yossel?" you challengingly asked when I said I'd rather kill myself than go to another Hebrew lesson. "What did the Eternal, Blessed be He, ask Yossel when he was dying?"

"His name," I said.

"What name?"

"His Hebrew name."

"And in what language did the Lord speak to Yossel"—you raised your voice—"in Hungarian?"

"In Hebrew," I would admit. I was in bed next to you. I had heard about him too—not God, Yossel.

"Then go!" You would push me out bodily while I screamed that I already knew my name and I was ready to die rather than go.

"Die then!" you would yell.

Even now, Mama, I'm still struggling with Hebrew. I can barely read even with the vowel signs, I haven't made much progress. Is it the fault of those first lessons? If Freud is right, the reason is there, it can never be taken away.

But don't worry; I'll be able to say what I have to when I need to. And I'll finally be able to tell my real last name that no one knows and that almost no one can pronounce in the country where I live. A last name that not even your son, Edy, and his only son use anymore—a last name that will die soon, even my uncle has cut off half of it.

I'm sorry that my brother and your grandchild don't carry Papa's name. Sometimes when I write them I find myself wondering to whom the letter is addressed. What does that beautiful, almost noble Hungarian name have to do with my family?

Then, to think that my Jewish name, Frumet or Frume—an observant Jew—would be Pia in Italian. What an inappropriate name! If I'm not careful, I might even forget it. A name wasted on me—who can't even remember the holidays. If I didn't read the newspapers, or hear announcements on TV, I'd even forget Yom Kippur!

"It's monstrous isn't it, Mama?"

"Yes." I hear your brief reply like a final verdict.

"My religion is writing," I say in defense. "Forgive me," I add, and I would also like to assure you that I never swear. Never say God doesn't exist. I respect the believer. The one who truly believes. As long as he lives his belief. I even envy him. Sometimes I could use a god myself. A prayer would do me good. At least I could fast on Yom Kippur the way so many Jews do who keep their stores open even on the Sabbath. The trouble is, I'm an extremist, I don't like compromises. If I fasted on Yom Kippur, I'd keep my store shut on Saturday. Do you know what happened to me last Yom Kippur? Rejoice! I ate and then threw up.

"You were punished," you reply promptly.

I admit that even I thought I'd been punished. Sometimes I realize that I'm thinking like you, walking and cooking like you—no, better than you, you were always too poor to cook well. Whatever you made, you were always missing some ingredient. I'm not lacking anything. I have more than I need. An excess.

"And don't you want to thank God?" you are asking me already.

"Where do you come from, who are you?" you would ask me—and yourself—when I didn't want to pray, or when I wanted to know why people had so many children if they couldn't support them. You see. Now you would have fewer dead children and I wouldn't be alive either. It's not that I don't enjoy life, but it's hard work, Mama—one isn't born because of merit, one doesn't die because of it either. Death selects like Mengele. I am my own Mengele! I don't know why I'm alive and not you, who would have prayed for everyone. You were my faith, now you're not here and I defend myself against every image that reminds me of faith—and of you. At Passover I didn't even want to see the matzos, because you were in that crisp, paper-thin bread. Now, I eat it along with leavened bread and ham! I'll go to hell for that, won't I?

"Yes," you answer calmly, convinced that I have to pay, that it's right to pay for your sins.

I haven't told you yet that the last time I went to temple, the pope was there.

Yes, yes, the pope. You don't believe me? I saw him with my own eyes. He shook my hand, I swear to you, and I never swear, Mama, believe me. You don't answer. Say nothing. How am I to interpret this? Forgive me, even though he is God on earth for the Christians, meeting him, I was moved and I imagined that he was going to tell me something extraordinary, divine, but instead he smiled at me, his mouth a little tight as if he were measuring his smiles, and with his Polish accent and a worldly ceremonious tone, all he said was, "Pleased to meet you," nothing more; he dropped my hand for another hand, gave a similar smile, repeated the same thing while the photographers' flashes were unleashed on this unique event in Judeo-Christian history.

During a pause, the chief rabbi of Rome and the pope were telling a sort of joke and laughing a lot as if nothing had happened between us during the last two thousand years. Though they were each wearing the uniform of their faith, they were simply acting like men. They resembled each other. The rabbi could have been Catholic, and the pope Jewish. And the guests, including me, Mama, were so humble, and happy and moved, as if we were the guilty ones and not the Church. The rabbi was happier than the pope and the Jews happier than the non-Jews, while the Romans couldn't understand what their foreign, too Polish pope was doing in a synagogue. They took it as one of the many visits he made as God's salesman always going around the world. One day with Pinochet, another with Waldheim, still another with the rabbi. Even the pope is promiscuous.

Listen to me, Mama, me who doesn't pray. It would take two thousand years of Christian prayer recited aloud to reestablish the original brotherhood. Or rather, the paternity that has been reviled, despised, denied, assassinated.

"Shh"—you want me to keep quiet. The world is changed, Mama. In Italy you can speak freely, it's a country of words, of popes, of compromises and contradictions—of yes and no at the same time, even the Roman Jews are a bit Catholic.

Am I crazy? Even Golda agrees and she says that a Jew can be really Jewish only in Israel.

I've lived in Israel too and I felt less Jewish there than anywhere else. Maybe because your fables didn't come true, nothing did, not even the stories I used to tell you when you cried and seemed so miserable. I used to believe in them a bit myself, telling you—when you could tolerate the sound of my voice—how I would be, grown-up, rich, and happy and would give you everything. You would live with me in a big city where even Papa wouldn't have to work anymore, and I wouldn't let you wash even a handkerchief, a sock, or a plate.

Sometimes your tears would turn into a half smile of pity for your dreaming child, deluded and, fortunately for her, totally unaware.

I would have kept my promises; even if I'm not so happy or so rich, you wouldn't have lacked for anything.

I was happy for a long time with Gabriele, my husband—not a Jew, not even a believer; he didn't even go with me to see the pope. Never went to Edy's or to see Golda in Israel or America.

He only came with me to one place, our village. When I met Gabriele—don't be upset, Mama—I loved him before I even knew his name or his religion. I wouldn't have cared if he'd been a Muslim instead of an unbaptized secularist, to me he was perfect just the way he was. He was a man. With a wounded look. A poet. Auschwitz was familiar to him. Poets are like prophets.

"All you do is read poetry," you scolded me daily, remember? I do. You would tear the book out of my hands and order me to stop dreaming, stop fantasizing, stop reading useless things instead of praying.

Ah Mama, without poetry, without art, nature, life would be unbearable. The air would be unbreathable. You don't know how much truth can be held in a single verse—a single word.

I, who knew whole books of poetry by heart, couldn't remember even one at Auschwitz. I forgot everything beautiful, as though it had never existed. I even forgot the songs, and I knew so many, was always singing or reading. Poetry and beauty must have abandoned me at the instant of my arrival at Auschwitz. That sight canceled both past and future, though you were still beside me, but for how long? Some quick steps. Ten? Twenty? An eternity? I don't know . . .

"Don't get scared, lower your head, just walk, walk!" I told myself as if I were entranced—drawn, drunk, struck by the horror, I staggered on among shouts and shoves, weapons and uniforms, cries and swoons, children strangled by their mothers.

"Where is Elsa, Leah, Miriam, Aron, your father! Golda?" You shook me, asking where they'd disappeared, where they'd gone to. You couldn't find them anymore, you didn't have your glasses. As if it were my fault that I couldn't find them either, that I confused them with other naked men and women. But when had I ever seen my father or my brother and sisters naked? I had never even seen you naked. Not even your breasts. Not your thighs. Not even your shoulders. You would slip from one piece of clothing to another behind the wardrobe door. It seemed like a crime to observe you. Almost as bad as eating ham, telling lies, or not respecting your parents. Or marrying a non-Jew. I am guilty of all these crimes, Mama, and many more.

"Smile if you like," you say, but you don't get angry. You don't leave me, you listen. I confess that although I was happy with Gabriele for a long time, I missed the rituals and holidays, the celebrations. He didn't like—still doesn't—birthdays, while I would have liked a life full of holidays, games, riddles, walks in the woods.

Contrary to what you might think, Mama—and to what I once thought—living with a nonbeliever is like living with a hermit. A righteous man. A moral example. A Franciscan who talked to a mouse that was lost in our first house. Who even talked to the ants on the wall near the sugar jar. His mother was that way too. And what a mother she was! She played Beethoven, translated Goethe, and always dressed in pale lilac or pure white.

Her body by then all bone, bent by age, was always draped in silk and cashmere. Her white hair was gathered under an invisible net that she never took off, even at night. I loved her. You weren't there. But hugging or kissing her wasn't easy. She even kept a slight distance from her children, who sometimes dared to rest a head on her lap or against her frail shoulder. But only the two males, Leonardo the eldest and Gabriele a few years younger. The daughter, Nora, never did it. And then, she—the goddess—would offer some affectionate gesture, a light caress or a modestly restrained smile. In comparison, Mama, we were Gypsies shouting our pains and joys to the four corners of the globe.

To Gabriele I must have seemed a barbarian who invaded his solitary life with my wild passions, my constant need for affection, sex, love, my need for him day and night—when he woke up, when he was walking, reading, eating, or taking a pee or a shit in the bathroom.

From the beginning of our relationship, Gabriele listened fascinated when I talked about you and me. Then he would disappear, sometimes for a few days. Was it to digest my story? Or to get away from me?

I didn't dare call him, but one night I spied on him in a little restaurant on a small street in the heart of Rome where I used to live alone in a furnished room. I still live there in an apartment where they are trying to evict me though I love my house so much I could die for it. I am prone to die for love.

So Gabriele was there. Sitting at the middle of a big table, apparently alone. Next to him there were some men and a single woman, a friend who that very evening was supposed to be with me consoling me for my great love for Gabriele and instead there she was with him. Oh the miserable woman! I could have killed her. What a traitor! Whore, piece of shit. What a despicable person. Sorry, Mama.

And he was talking, eating his usual plate of roast veal with potatoes, drinking his red wine with gusto, forgetting all about me. Content. Self-sufficient. He was fine! While I was in a helpless frenzy. Unable to contain the cry that drew a little crowd of passersby, who at that time were not monkeys unable to hear or speak but were still human beings.

"What's the matter? What is it?" everyone asked. "What can I do for you?" And they offered to take me wherever I needed to go, invited me to their houses, offered me real handkerchiefs, asked me what country I came from and if I had family in Italy, if I needed anything—what could they do?

"Nothing, nothing," I stammered.

"Have you lost someone?" They worried and made the sign of the cross.

"No no no," I repeated, retreating so far that I lost myself.

I lose myself easily and often. I lose myself everywhere. I don't recognize myself even in my street, where between one day and the next there is a new shop in place of the old one. Between one day and the next I forget what there used to be in the new windows full of suits, of shoes and furs and designer coats.

The only place where I've been able to orient myself even after twenty years of absence is our native village, Mama. I've been back to our house twice. The first time our house was still standing and Gabriele came too. The second time I was by myself. The house was a ruin. They shot a film in Hungary about my life and they destroyed the house in the film itself when I was no longer there.

Don't tell me I shouldn't have done the film, I had to. To tell about you, all of you, to tell the story that isn't taught at school. The young people today don't even know who Che Guevara is.

Many people remembered you in the village, remembered your coming and going in the courtyard. Your beauty. Your fear of God. Papa. The poor Jew who was a bit like them. I even saw Lenke. Do you remember Lenke, Mama? My best friend. The daughter of the widow who drank. The last one to stop seeing me—and then I stopped wanting to live. She'd gotten fat, she seemed older than me, and she's still jealous because I was better than she was in school, because I live in the West and am happy.

I also saw our dear Mari. She is so old, Mama! A mummy who cried as she showered me with kisses, saliva and tears, food and memories: "Katia, Katia, Katia," she intoned as if I were dead, then asked about you as if I'd seen you yesterday, as if you had remained at home.

"And your mother?" So many of the villagers asked, wanting to know how you were, where you were. Either they didn't believe what they'd seen, or didn't believe the unbelievable, or didn't want to remember your death.

In our once dark and muddy village, one day washing machines arrived. The tractor. In the evening no one spins by gaslight anymore, no one sings love songs—there is the radio to listen to, the television to dream with.

The young people wear jeans and love everything that comes from the West. They don't remember anything. They don't know about you or me—about our house or the one tree still alive in our garden.

They don't know where the synagogue was, the first that was destroyed. They didn't care at all about the Hebrew cemetery full of nettles and shit and other filth.

On Grandma's tomb, your mother's, I found an overturned chamber pot.

Today maybe nothing is left. There is no trace of us. We never existed and will never exist.

Gabriele cried too when he saw our village, our house still standing. For the film I went alone and was more alone than I'd ever been. They told me that the municipality had registered my name, the date of my birth, Papa's name, the date of your birth but not your deaths.

"The television is here!" The village's most extraordinary news obscured even the presence of the film troupe.

"Television," they all said, and I, who cannot stand television, must have grimaced. I still write by hand. Like a scribe. That's the only way I can delude myself that I've left some written document. Like our ancestors.

A typed manuscript leaves no traces of self, the letters are all the same, errors disappear, everything disappears, the errors, the erasures, the reticence and self-censure, the blood, the pain of writing. When Gabriele sees me writing by hand in my notebook on my knee, he repeats, "You'll never change." And he is moved and frightened by such faithfulness to everything as if I were a phenomenon outside time.

"If only I could," I sigh, and he knows what I am trying to say and I know how he'd answer, what he doesn't say, I can guess what he is looking for, the name he cannot remember.

I'm a little bit of a seer, like you, Mama. Better than the fortune-tellers who go around Rome and earn more than a university professor.

I went to one of them too, I even went to the horoscope reader who lives like a king, I went to everyone but a magician!

The woman with the cards talked to me about you. And Papa. When I turned the card with the figure of death, she said it was you. She must have gotten everything she said from me, because she guessed it all: another woman in Gabriele's life, another man by my side, work that I'd waited for, unexpected fortune, a slight illness.

"You have two children," she asserted mistakenly, and the game was up. Too bad. In those moments, one can also have faith in the cards.

You know I have no children. How could I bring one into the world after your end? I've always aborted them, Mama. Here's another reason to disown me. My first unwanted child now would have had children and I would already be a grandmother. Fortunately Gabriele didn't long to be a father—a child, a poet, jealous of his time and his solitude.

I'm not sorry I aborted, Mama, even if I'm unworthy of you, eight times a mother by the will of the Lord.

If I had a daughter, maybe she would be like Sara, the beautiful Sara who sucked the milk of Auschwitz and who has a sort of resistance in her splendid eyes—a hostility toward life similar to that of my friend, a great Italian writer, who committed suicide a short while ago.

In Golda's son's eyes, instead, life sparkles. It burns. And it is the same thing.

You have great-grandchildren now, Mother. Four. If you could only see them you'd be a happy great-grandma. They're healthy. Beautiful. Perfect. They're still children. Who will ever tell them our story? No one. They'll learn something vague at school. On anniversaries maybe they'll take a bunch of flowers to the monuments, they'll start to play and, while playing, to decipher the strange foreign names. Auschwitz, Treblinka, Bergen-Belsen . . .

Golda loves her children too much, but how could you? You had so many of them. She lives for her children, she has remarried for them, she lives in America with her suitcase always ready to rejoin them at the least stirring of nostalgia for them, for Israel. For Golda not even America is America. I saw her a little while ago in New York. She seemed like one of your sisters, all apron and anxiety, joy and laments. She waited for me in the street. A street like those you find in a small and clean town, in a pretty district with identical houses, gardens, and garages. She kissed me over and over and made me eat and eat again, and she cried. She cries every time she sees me come and again when I go. She almost comes with me the way she did when they separated me from her in Auschwitz. And before taking leave of each other we look at each other for a moment, our breathing suspended, eyes remembering.

Golda's refrigerator is like a store, Mama. It is filled with every imaginable goody, as though there were ten people instead of two, or better, as if she were alone, always waiting for someone to arrive or leave.

Golda doesn't feel well anywhere, only when she is traveling, as in the story of the old Jew who is always setting out.

Gabriele likes Golda. He says she is a wild thing, a rock, a force of nature, a beautiful woman with two eyes of black fire.

But she confessed to me that she tires easily. Is short of breath. She smokes too much, like me. She worries about the future of her children, of her grandchildren. At sixty, she studies English. She has learned to drive and goes around the neighborhood visiting her fellow countrymen, cousins, deportees, new arrivals from Israel, Israelis who are going back home.

She's become blond, mother! That Gypsy. Her husband was afraid that she'd be mistaken for a Portuguese.

Golda says that everyone is crazy in America, crazier than in other places, also stupider, they only care about money, are always quoting figures, what did this or that cost—dollars, dollars, dollars.

As soon as she sees me, she asks, "Do you remember, do you remember?"

And she sets off talking about how and when we escaped death and who she's met from Auschwitz, or Bergen-Belsen or Dachau.

A sinister nostalgia throbs in her dark black eyes; they shine with the force, the triumph of a survivor.

She is even attracted to death, maybe yours, maybe of all those who didn't come back. Every once in a while she thinks of suicide the way she did back then. She has passed this on to her daughter. Sometimes I too think that I'm tired, that I ought to be done with life. The last time the sick idea came to me was the eve of Passover when my writer-friend, also a survivor, killed himself. He was the witness most listened to, loved, esteemed, read. If he did it, I cried out at the betrayal—what pain, what paralyzing stupor—I could do it too. Who knows what wounded him more, the past or the future. Auschwitz or those who denied it happened.

I even considered not writing anymore. If his voice was extinguished, what use was mine? If he permitted himself to commit suicide, I could permit myself to do it too.

Then I met two women, one in Rome and one in Canada. Two survivors. The Canadian never leaves her house for fear of being seen, taken away. Her daughter tells her she's right. She too has sucked the milk of Auschwitz, like Sara, but Golda isn't paranoid.

The Hungarian tourist in Rome, at a supper for two, was looking over her shoulder, advising me to be attentive—one could be taken anywhere, without warning.

What pain, Mama, what pain. You think it's easy being a survivor?

The Canadian showed me her childhood notebook where everything is written down in case she disappears. The Hungarian, who knows my name because she's seen the film on my life, convinced me to continue to write for them. "If you like, I'll tell you my story," she offered, speaking quickly as if she was going to die that very night.

"I know, I know." I tried to stop the wave of tears that fell continually from eyes that seem much older than mine though we were the same age. Maybe she aged so much because she could neither talk nor write. Silence ate away her skin, her flesh. "I have an adopted daughter," she told me, trying to get my approval or disapproval. "She's a Gypsy. The best child that I know. She loves me. She's grateful to me. I put her through school. She is a nurse. She already has a child. I'm a grandmother. The little girl is six years old. She dreams of having a Barbie, the doll! She wants her blond, with a spare set of clothes. It's too expensive, how can I buy it for her? Will you give it to me as a present?" "Yes, yes, I'll get it for you," I said, and she suddenly stopped crying.

How would you have lived afterward, Mama? Would you still have prayed? Said that only God knows what He's doing? That only He could answer my questions. I would have fought with you. Would we have kept fighting forever? You would never have approved of anything I did. I would have done everything suffering double. You would have stopped speaking to me the way you did when I was little. And it was worse than reproaches or threats or some blow or slap for something I'd done, because I'd provoked it, hadn't I? In your silences there was something mean, dangerous. Your clear eyes darkened like daylight in midday obscured by a sudden cloud.

You didn't love me anymore, it would have been better if I hadn't been born. You heaped all your sorrows on me—as a wife, as a mother, as a Jew. Behind your closed mouth there were five thousand years of brutal history. Do you think I didn't read it in your look even if I was ignorant of the details?

And after all this I still dared to laugh, play, run, hope.

When I looked at you, I said to myself, "Poor Mama. She's old. She can't remake herself. I have a whole life ahead of me. To repair the world the way you'd repair a cart or a stuck plow or a pot with a hole in it."

When I told you that I wasn't going to have your life, you preferred not to talk to me again, not even to greet me when I came back from school. Throwing down a plate with some leftovers: "Here, dreamer, you're so smart, come down to earth!" or you didn't say anything. You didn't notice me, looked beyond me like Mengele the selector.

Gabriele was sorry not to have known you, Mama. He smiled ruefully, the way you do when you are expecting someone who changes her mind at the last minute.

If you were alive would you have come with me to Edy's, to Golda? Where would you have lived? You would never have come to us in Rome. In my house where the menorah has a prominent place, there is smoked ham . . .

Only imagine you and my mother-in-law together! Could there be anything stranger? You would have studied each other, sniffed like two dogs meeting each other. She purebred, you a mongrel. You a little stout in dark clothes with your moon face, kerchief of an observant Jew on your head, she thin, aristocratic, secular, a goddess in white who would have been taller than you by a head.

But this doesn't mean that she was better than you, Mama, don't misunderstand. Don't be jealous. You are worth as much as she, more, with your life so incomparably more difficult.

She liked you too. She was a mother. Not far from death. She liked to hear me talking about you, she listened as if I were telling a dark tale. When she tired, early as always, she would start—in her silent, civic indignation, a fastidious blinking of her eyes that stopped my tongue in mid-sentence. Somewhat hurt and tender, I would stay there in silence looking at the beautiful old lady so full of dignity.

You know that she even named me in her short will? Among the few things she left, there were five gold pieces for me, three strings of antique coral, a child's pearl necklace. In addition, I took some things with no material value: a pair of white slippers that she wore on her thin feet; I can still see the way she walked lamely with her stick toward her destination, the white sofa where she would sit down wearily, humiliated by the pains of age. Hurriedly adjusting her handmade shawl, her dress with the skirt that reached her ankles, which, like some abbess, she covered with white stockings. Everyone, not just I the foreign daughter-in-law, was intimidated by her, even her children. Leonardo the architect, Gabriele the poet, and Nora the one-time seamstress all full of life and chatter. She talked just to talk. In order to dream, to believe in her dreams—riches, beauty, eternal youth. She was the opposite of her mother the way Golda's daughter is of her mother. Nora, who didn't want to get old, died at barely sixty, carefully coiffed and made up, with her sparse hair still untouched by the illness.

With morphine in her body instead of cobalt (it was decided not to humiliate her with a treatment that would give her only a few more days to live) she dreamed right up to the end. She was realizing her old wish to go to Mexico with her brother Leonardo, who had just presented her with a jewel for the trip and would pay for all the expenses as he always did out of innate generosity as well as duty, because he was the eldest son and they had lost their father so young.

The difference between us and them is enormous, Mama. The older members of this bourgeois family and the newly born almost never see each other. They never talk among themselves, never cry. I see my faraway relatives more than they see each other living in the same town, the same city, at a distance of twenty minutes that at times seems insuperable.

I miss having Gabriele's family. I miss their Christmas, which they didn't celebrate, though they got together for a dinner and exchanged little packages with bows. We all became like children and like children ran to open our gifts and oh what lovely stockings, what a pretty pullover, what a nice purse, what handsome ties, what a beautiful antique jewel for me—who loves everything that shines and has colored stones.

Forgive me, Mama, I'm naming names that don't mean anything to you. Gabriele doesn't regret those Christmases lost after the death of his mother, of his sister, his uncles and aunts. He doesn't love ceremonies as I do. He gives me pres-

ents all year long, perhaps to feel guilt-free? But a trip would
be too much and he has never gone to Edy's. Edy lives in
Brazil. Have I already told you that? I might repeat myself.
Who doesn't? Edy has worked all his life for his modest
riches and now can't enjoy them. He's had a heart attack.
Still he enjoys his beloved son, his two grandchildren. He
has six pure-blooded dogs, twenty chickens, a carriage, and
a swimming pool that a black man is always cleaning.

Edy is a good Jew, Mama, the kind you like. He is always for Israel and donates an amount every month. He
doesn't live there, however, though he did live there for a
long time. He has a rich man's place in the most beautiful
synagogue of São Paulo; the community has given him a
decoration in the name of Israel. You would forgive him
everything, wouldn't you? He too eats ham. And when
he smoked, he smoked even on Saturday the way Papa
did in secret. And he drives too on Saturday, like the uncle who keeps kosher. Edy nourishes himself more with
pills than with food, he has to measure everything, he
is always dieting and always wants to eat—he's always
hungry, he has a ferocious hunger.

His grandchildren, already adolescents, don't know
about Auschwitz. Who would have dared to tell them
anything—happy and gay, almost as if they weren't Jews.
Being Jewish is natural to them, they even go to a Hebrew
school that teaches them something, maybe the little that

they have to know. The tattoo on their grandfather's arm was intriguing to play with, they have always seen it. It's as natural as a mole. Edy wanted so much to see Gabriele in his beautiful house in São Paulo. I did too.

They've always come to visit us, or I went to them alone like a widow or a divorcee. When they came here, Gabriele wasn't stingy with his attention and seductive warmth. He even loved them, and why not? After conquering them he would shrug his shoulders timidly and excuse himself, fleeing early.

It was my brother. My sister-in-law. Our things. What mattered to him always was his time, his space, his freedom, at any cost.

Poets are egotistical, Mama. Like all creative people. Gabriele is an innocent with all his faults. I too.

Golda and Edy like Gabriele. They love him. They greet him in all their letters. They never forget him. Maybe because he's my husband and husbands must be respected. By law.

"A kiss to Gabriele," they write me. "Greetings to Andrea too," they add wearily.

Edy is a bit taciturn, like Papa. He looks like him. Fatter. More cheerful. He's a rich man. With a wonderful, patient, slavish wife, who serves him like a king. I love him a lot, Mama. He's a good brother. A good man. Simple. Generous. But he too chooses who to give to and who not.

With Edy I become part daughter, part sister. We laugh, sing, joke together. He treats me to everything, even the journey, acting the male part, the father, the part of the older brother with his younger sister who doesn't work, who writes.

I like playing the playful child with men, maybe because Papa was never around and then just wasn't there anymore.

Edy too cries when he sees me arrive alone and leave alone. We are always crying with the joy of seeing each other again and the fear that it will be for the last time. This is why when we're together, we are always together, as much as we possibly can be. Golda even comes into the bathroom with me the way she did when we were children; we bathe together in a bathtub, not in a basin heated by the sun.

Gabriele can't understand our relationship. He can't understand how we can stay together so much. What can we talk and talk about, smoking on and on like mad.

Edy also gets angry when we smoke so much, like everyone who has stopped smoking. He's a fanatic, like all converts.

His house is so clean and antiseptic that I almost hide my smoking, I walk attentively, sit down with caution. Immediately replace anything I've disturbed. Don't touch anything, admire Edy's collection of horses and his wife's crystal.

Edy is sixty-two, Mama! When you saw him last, he was nineteen. What a handsome boy. Thin, smiling, always ready to fall in love, to sing. And while he sang, he would repair with his pricked tailor's fingers Papa's trousers and your horrible overcoat that lasted forever. Where did you get that coat, first lengthened then shortened, turned inside out and then turned again? And that man's hat you are wearing on your head in the Budapest photograph. Luckily I have another photo that I'm in too, the only one where we're together. Oddly, you have your head uncovered, without a scarf. How come? Confronting the camera, you gave up your faith for an instant, and how do you think I could keep mine when I faced Auschwitz?

In the other photo you have such an enigmatic smile, incredibly sweet. They should have photographed you forever to discover your thousand faces. You ought to have been an actress, Mama. Ahh . . . what am I saying, mmm? If it were possible you'd cut out my tongue, cut off my hand so I'd stop writing, isn't that so?

Edy has dark, smooth hair, fine without any white strands, just like Papa's. And he wears his hair the same way, divided on the side, slicked down like Rudolph Valentino's. Your son is vain, Mama. Even now, anyone who messes up his hair is in trouble. He wears made-to-order shirts, changes his linen and his tie every morning. He seems to have become shorter, he's gotten fat, too fat for his sick heart.

The name of his only son is Shalom, like his grandpa's, your husband. He has his father's voice, his mother's beautiful teeth and eyes—his whole way of being and moving is his father's. He is taller, more worldly, more cultured, more intelligent, and self-confident even though before settling down he moved so often. He was born in Hungary, attended elementary school in Israel, high school in Argentina, the university in Brazil. He too is a merchant, for his father's sake, and because he fell in love, married, and has two wonderful children and a wife who loves him. He's a happy man. Your great-grandchildren are even happier. They know nothing about their great-grandfather, very little about their grandfather.

Golda's daughter Sara is divorced, Mama. I didn't want to tell you. Golda will be angry at me for having written it to you. She is still in mourning for her daughter, who lives alone with her son Ariel, a superior being whom Golda loves like an orphan—oh, these young people who divorce and marry as if it all were a game.

"Poor little one," I've heard Golda say looking at Ariel. "Without a father and with a mother who works." She sighs, as if Ariel's father were dead and it were a crime for a mother to work.

And you'd better not contradict her. She's like you. She's your daughter. I sometimes seem a stranger to her, just as I did to you, although we're sisters and you were my mother.

Golda is like you even toward animals. I have two cats, and her daughter Sara has a dog and a rabbit. All of them irritate her. She can't understand how anyone can love an animal. Live with animals. Sleep with animals. Find their hair everywhere, even in the soup. However, she recognizes that animals are more loyal than people and perhaps even superior to them. She understands but doesn't dare admit it, she needs her morality, the faith that keeps her together. What a shame, Mama, that you never really knew animals—my cats. I treat them like two dear friends, I even say excuse me when I bump into them by accident. I talk to them the way you talked to me, to all of us.

"Don't you see? Are you blind? Do you have to be always underfoot? You never let me work in peace. Go on. Go play a little."

You're smiling? With pity for me? It offends you that I treat my animals like children? They are children, Mama.

"Poor thing," you comment to yourself, "she doesn't have children." If I told you that I have my books, you'd be scandalized. How can you compare a book to a son? A dead thing made out of paper to something living and sacred made of flesh and blood.

But books too are made of blood and flesh, Mama. Especially mine, they're not just mental products.

I know that you don't understand what I'm talking about. And I'm sorry. No one will ever understand the urgency I feel when I can't do anything but write—must write. Maybe writing is like an attack of madness, of uncontainable neurosis. Maybe it is nothing else, but for the one writing, it is everything.

Most times when I'm writing I forget everything, even to eat. I neglect the house. My dearest ones, the whole world, my nails, my hair, my body, the thousand other things I have to do.

I write. Smoke. Even hold back my pee. I'm disturbed by telephone calls, voices outside, my daily duties, the meows of the cats tired of seeing me writing instead of being with them, petting them, chatting a little. Jealous of my work. Animals are like artists: egotists and egoists.

Instead of truly listening to me, you only tolerate what I'm saying to you. I feel it. You don't think I'm normal, do you? Because I love my cats more than you love your children. I caress them, reassure them, never insult them. Never curse them. Never drive them away from me.

If you had loved me like that, I'd be happier today. Sara too would have been happier if her mother had loved her well; loving well is difficult for a mother.

Survivor mothers are extremists, they love too much, say too much, or don't say anything, they are always making mistakes. I would have made mistakes too. If I'd been a mother, when and how would I have told my children about Mengele?

And what would have been the right age to tell—
and up to what point—about an absolute injustice that
is beyond words. One is almost ashamed of one's own
suffering.

Should it be told little by little, measuring out the poison, or all at once, overwhelming the child's spirit?

How can you tell a child that his mother is alive by a
miracle, because everything was done to eliminate her?
The child, if too little, would ask what his mother did
wrong, how could she have been so bad that they wanted
to kill her? The mother would have to defend herself,
justify herself, explain that she wasn't bad, she was innocent, that the bad ones were the Nazis. But what does
Nazism signify to a child? It would be necessary to find
adequate parallels for a child, calling them the bogey-
man, the big bad wolf, the devil, or who knows what,
and then it all would become a story for him, even if an
unattractive one that he wouldn't like and whose sequel
he wouldn't want to know.

If she told the child that they wanted to kill her for the
simple reason that she was Jewish, and that they wanted
to kill all the Jews, the child would ask automatically what
harm the Jews did—him included, because he is Jewish.

And guilt would insinuate itself along with a sense of in-
security and fear for her own life, for the life of her mother
and father and brothers—for all the Jewish people.

I know of children who asked their mothers why they are Jewish and of mothers who answered that there is nothing wrong in being Jewish, that some people are born Jewish, some Christian, some Muslim or something else.

"And did the wicked Nazis also want to kill the Christians and the Muslims?" asked a child of my acquaintance.

The mother quickly said no, they only wanted to kill the Jews. While she said it, she opened her eyes wide with a mixture of indignation and vindication, like someone who has had a privilege, something more in life, not less.

Is it possible to be proud of one's suffering as one is of one's achievements? I don't know. Maybe, yes. I've never met a survivor who said he would have liked to have been born a pure Arian. Although many Jews have assimilated, others have distanced themselves with some ideological excuse, and there are even anti-Semite Jews. Still others have made mixed marriages and their children are Catholics if the mother is Catholic or Jewish if the mother is Jewish—and this not because of Jewish law but because of the women, who are stronger and more insistent than the men.

As far as Gabriele was concerned, our son, if we ever had one, could even have become a rabbi, if that was my wish. Anything would have been fine for the sort of believer he was.

And what would I have done? I would have raised him like myself, a good secular Jew. I would have told him everything about myself, enriched him with my experience. He would have become wiser, more just, freer than I am, and who knows if he would have believed in God? I wouldn't have forbidden him anything. I would never have told him that there is a heaven and hell, that a man is all good or all bad. I wouldn't have told him about a chosen people and a holy land, only about people and countries and people without countries.

I would have told him that I had such a believer for a mother and lived in a world that was so full of faith and so hellish that I couldn't believe, even though I often felt the lack of faith the way a cripple feels the lack of his missing crutch.

Who knows what else I would have told him, how I would have ruined him? Mothers love their children but at times they forget to ask them what the children want or think, who they are and how they see the world.

And don't tell me that Jews are better. Auschwitz notwithstanding, Jews are like everyone else. Nothing more. If you say they're better, it's like denying that they're human beings, no better or worse than others, even if others see them as different. And they're judged differently when they kill, throw phosphorus bombs, sneak up on the enemy, attack first, become guerrillas, kidnap people, torture prisoners, just as everyone else does for reasons of state, in the name of patriotism. I am talking about

Israelis, not us Diaspora Jews, we don't have to stain our hands and spirits for our country, we're outsiders, even though—for as long as Jews have been judged—we're judged en masse, one for all and all for one. The government of the State of Israel doesn't consult us, doesn't in fact listen to anyone, is deaf to complaints, doesn't see beyond its nose—or pretends not to see. Who knows what game they are playing that will come out of our hides? Would you like Israel? And the Israelis? If you saw the way they are, you wouldn't believe your eyes, you'd lose your faith in Moses's Ten Commandments.

Contradictions are at the source of all faith, Mama. How do you conquer a country, inhabited for thousands of years, if not by arms? How do you make a just division after you have conquered it by dying and killing? There is too much blood involved, too many great differences, too little goodwill and even less humility. People who have been humiliated too much are not inclined to concede anything even to those who have had nothing to do with their humiliation.

But there's a place for everyone in this world, Mama, you just have to move over a bit, draw back a little. And you can even overcome hunger if you give everyone what's superfluous. What a lovely dream—so simple, isn't it? But it isn't realizable, because a man is only a man, little more than nothing.

If you want to know, in Israel your bearded Jews, the Orthodox models you held up against my father, are a minority. They are the different ones. They live by the law and are treated as outlaws. And this too is the price of living in a country where things are bought and sold even on Saturday. Where life can't stop even for a single day, where there are no goyim to turn off the light, start the fire, carry the weights. Doctors can't refuse to operate on Saturdays, nurses give injections, soldiers have to kill, cars keep going.

How could the Sabbath be celebrated in Israel? Don't you see, it's all a contradiction.

Israelis are allergic to beards. Do you know what I heard a child in Jerusalem say when he saw an Orthodox man? "Papa, Papa, look, there's a Jew!" And he said it in Hebrew.

Would you ever have said such a thing? Ever believed it? I've seen Israeli soldiers on television attacking the Orthodox and vice versa.

Don't get mad at me, it's not my fault. I wish it weren't true. I'd rather not have seen it myself. Don't transfix me with your eyes like that, I'm innocent. I didn't kill anyone. And there's no longer any danger that I will. I let slip the best occasions. I couldn't kill. Is that my religion? Who knows if it's more honorable to kill or be killed. If the hero is the one who shoots or the victim who falls. Whatever the truth of it, I can only be a victim.

You educated me, Mama. I'm the result of your teaching. Didn't you tell me that a Jew never kills anyone, doesn't even raise his voice, that it's best if he walks on tiptoe not letting anyone know he exists? This was the game I played with Mengele. The invisibility game. I was there and he didn't see me. Because I didn't want to be seen. Is it thanks to you that I'm alive? Not to Golda. To whom do I owe the luck of being and not being?

When Mengele came during the roll call and began to select, I squinted furtively at him and said to myself, God, don't let him see me, I'm not here, I don't exist, he can't see me, he mustn't see me, he won't see me! And I saw him, he was there, and I pulled in my stomach with all my force and told myself that he didn't see me, mustn't see me, that his horrible eyes had to fall on someone else.

Nice game, wasn't it? What a nice wish! That's how it was, Mama. It's the truth. If they reduce you to a hungry animal, you become a hungry animal. Would you have stayed yourself? You rarely gave in, you always won— with us, with Papa—you were always right. Who knows if you would have lowered your head to the club without cursing or returning the blow? I can't imagine you reduced to a lamb, you who were a tigress, a lioness—one who roared.

Golda and Edy will be outraged for what I've dared to do, Mama. But like you, they want the impossible. That I be the way you were—like them. They are upset because I've broadcast the fact that we were poor.

Shameful, isn't it? But what's to be ashamed of? Did we steal? Is it the poor man who ought to be ashamed of his poverty or is it the rich man who sees it? What do you say? Nothing? Is everything a result of the divine will? You're joking, Mama. If everyone had your faith, there'd never be any progress and the poor would accept their poverty without complaint, evangelically or Hebraically.

Oh forgive me, Mama, a thousand times, forgive me. You are one of the holy dead, an untouchable martyr— true, but it's also true that you're my mother. And I've the right to tell my mother everything. In fact, I have to.

You aren't just the mother of Edy and Golda. You are also mine and if I don't talk to you, say your name, fight with you, I forget you, and if I don't write about you, I'll let you be forgotten.

And if I forget you, I forget myself. As long as I exist, you do too. Only death will cut the cord. Don't you feel me in your womb? Can't you hear my heart beating? If you don't hear me, then you no longer hear anything.

Oh how serious you are. How silent. Couldn't you ever give me a sign of life? Tell me I have everything wrong. Accuse me, deceive me if you want to but make me believe once more in your yes and your no. Tell me a story. A true one. You've never told me one. A story never came from your mouth. Only judgments. Truths. Threats. Sinister forbodings. But faith, for the love of God! Such faith! Honesty. Humility. Resignation.

According to you, either someone believes or he should cut his throat before someone else cuts it.

Nonetheless, I didn't kill myself the way my dear friend did who hadn't been educated by a mother like you. He was an Italian in Italy, in his country. An Italian Jew. As for me, when can I say I'm something before being Jewish? I don't know if he killed himself first as an Italian and then as a Jew or vice versa. I suspect that he killed himself because he was a Jew. And because he was a Jew, they deported him. There is always a moment in which a Jew is only a Jew—deprived of his secular citizenship in a flash.

Why did he kill himself? Why? No one knows, Mama. It's a mystery. Something unknown.

With him too, I talked about you. I even showed him your photograph. Both of them. The one where we were together and the other of you in Budapest where the same white collar shows from under your coat and you're holding your borrowed purse in your hand.

"What a beautiful face," he said. "Your mother is beautiful," he added timidly and looked at me as if to say that I was beautiful too.

"You're good-looking too," I said and he turned away his perpetually uneasy glance, held prisoner in a secret duel, veiled by false serenity.

Golda's daughter Sara has the same look although she was never in Auschwitz but only sucked its milk.

"Don't let yourself go," I used to say to him, with utter banality, when he sometimes let a complaint escape him on the phone.

"I'm depressed. I'm afraid of not being able to write. I won't write anymore."

"Oh come on," I'd joke, "we're indestructible. And we'll always write. We'll keep on forever." I tried to play down those sensations that every writer feels. And I would have liked to add some further silliness just to provoke a smile on that overly discreet mouth of his. I would have given anything to open a way out in his mind, which was being drawn into the vortex of his depression—if he'd asked me, I would have fasted on Yom Kippur.

But he didn't fast either. He was too much a Piedmontese, too bourgeois for my Gypsy heart.

Piedmontese Jews are like Piedmontese, Mama, different from Roman Jews, who are like other Romans. Roman Jews seem like Gypsies compared with the Jews from Piedmonte.

The Roman Jew is vulgar, suspicious, and talkative; the Piedmontese is closed off, cold, courteous.

Did you know you were beautiful? Did you ever look at yourself in the mirror out of vanity? I never saw you in the wardrobe mirror or in that little mirror where Papa shaved his beard. I looked at myself in the glass of the door and you scolded me as though I'd committed a crime.

In the photo taken in Budapest next to your daughter Mara, a radiant bride, you have the sweetest smile. A smile that I'd never seen. Is it possible? Our cousin Anna is beautiful too. If you could only see her now. She seems like someone else. Only her goodness has remained unchanged, but it didn't do her much good, on the contrary she paid too much for life. Luckily she has children who love her and stay close.

On your right, in the photo, there's another cousin, on your side, not Papa's—a nasty bunch, you said, with hearts like stone. Then there is your eldest daughter, Leah, her beautiful face deformed—by the camera lens? an abscess? a malign shadow? At your shoulder the end of a tree-lined street, beyond you the facade of a synagogue, a theater, a museum? The enlargement has blurred everything and turned you all a sepia rose color.

Even though I've been to the mythical city of Budapest several times since then—kneeling the first time I saw it, after the war—I never found that corner, Mama, and I continue to ask myself where it is. Where are you, Mama? With your coat patched a thousand times, badly made, ugly and dark, that deformed and hid you. You have on your only pair of good shoes, tight on your swollen feet. And that miserable purse in your hand. Who lent it to you? I never saw it at home. It wasn't there. I'm sure. How many times I rummaged around in your meager things. How many times I put them on in secret: your clothes, your shoes with heels, your cotton slip, your aprons. One time I even dared touch your face powder that had been there for years in a little cardboard box decorated with colored flowers on a dark ground. Oh what a perfume that rosy powder had—magical, eternal, almost never used. Relics of your buried femininity.

In the photo on either side your two nieces press close to you. They are my cousins, the daughter of one of your many saintly brothers and the daughter of one of Papa's many sisters, not one of the arid spinsters but the nicest and the poorest. They cling to you, you cling to no one, you are alone, standing straight. Maybe this moment caught by the camera was your only moment of independent existence.

"They're elegant," comments Gabriele whenever he looks at the photograph. "They seem like bourgeois citizens. What was your mother doing in Budapest?" he unfailingly adds.

"I've already told you, she went for the wedding of my sister Mara. Don't you remember? It was the only trip she took . . ." I sighed impatiently, like you, Mama, with us. Like you, disappointed.

But what can your one trip to Budapest mean to Gabriele? What to me was important, sacred even, was only a bit of information to him or anyone else, quickly forgotten, not even registered. And that's normal, Mama. Everyone is alone with his life and his memories. Even I can't know what his vacations with his mother in Brianza or Levanto meant to Gabriele. I don't even know where Levanto is and I've never seen the Brianza region. I just barely know Milan, where he was born and grew up; I can't even orient myself in Rome, Mama. Cities make people lose themselves, friends, neighbors, tenants on the same floor. The city divides, distances, and consumes people.

I only know our village well—the mysterious and frightening wood where I picked the first flowers for you, where I played hide-and-seek and mommy-and-daddy— where the paths were muddy, the houses white with red roofs, where the women wore black and the men black rags and everything smelled of marmalade, hay, cattle, flowers, and lilac. Do you remember Gabor? The youngest child of Vago? My classmate? The idiot! I saw him again.

You used to say that only a fool like him would play with a Jew. But Gabor wasn't a fool, Mama, only too poor to be considered normal. He courted me. From one of the many holes in his ragged pants, he set himself to urinate like a virtuoso, designing a heart, his, for me in the winter snow or summer dust. Or a flower for me. Or a little boy, himself, for me. Hurriedly, for fear he'd run out of urine or I'd disappear, he made a circle for a head, a horizontal line for the body, two short arms, two legs with bare feet and then he'd laugh happily and I'd laugh too looking at that ruddy thing sticking out of his pants like a peeled, boiled carrot.

He wasn't even ugly, Mama, it was poverty that made him ugly, made him awkward and even saddened the little thing with which he wrote me messages of love. True, he often had a snotty nose, and he wiped it—when he did—on the sleeve of his patched and dirty jacket.

When I saw him again as an adult, Mama, I found him handsome, tender, plumpish, with the rosy cheeks he had as a child.

He recognized me right away and embraced me. Stammered something. I, on the other hand, was trying to make out who he was. Who were the people calling me, pronouncing your name instead of mine?

"Do you remember, do you remember?" they asked, all of them crying, and I, while I said yes, that I remembered, remembered things of no importance, maybe about school, or urinating in the snow, or maybe the woods, the breakwater, the sheaves of hay, the games we played together, the baths we took in the river Tisza in the summer, the winter ice.

How many times you scolded me when I returned from one of my escapades, breathless from so much play, cold, my clothes dirty, my already damaged shoes ruined, my stomach so empty I could eat a horse.

"Make yourself even hungrier!" you protested. "Going in the woods with the boys. Nice thing for a girl! I'll break your legs! I'll tell your father. I'll kill you!"

"I was only playing," I would defend myself guiltily. "Can't a person even play?"

"All you do is play, instead of thinking."

"What should I think about?" I would ask in deadly earnest, frightened by the idea of thinking about serious things.

"Life," you'd say, giving a mortal weight to the word.

"Life?" I'd ask wonderingly, because for me life was just there and that was it, it was the other things that weren't there.

"Soon we'll have to look for a husband for you," you'd say slowly, sighing.

"A husband!" I was horrified. "I'm never going to marry someone I don't know, Mama, and don't love, never, never. I'd rather never get married."

"You've made some good choices"—you pause, restraining yourself—"running after love all your life. Marrying and divorcing and marrying again."

"I'm not just your daughter, Mama," I told you. "When I grow up I'll also be a woman. Weren't you ever a woman, not just daughter and mother?"

"I . . . woman?" you murmured, almost smiling as if I'd said something ridiculous or shameful.

Who knows if you understand what an orgasm is, Mama. It makes you forget the world. It permits moments of total absence. Of being raised above the earth. It's like flying, Mama. Maybe it's God.

But sexual passion is brief, Mother. The truth is what's left afterward, like gold washed from gravel. Something immutable paid for with blood and tears.

Don't close your ears, Mama. We're both grown women. You're ninety-three years old!

Try to understand me as a woman, a human being, not just your daughter, even if I too see you only as a mother. Children also tend to forget that their mother is a woman. A person can be a terrible wife and an excellent mother or vice versa. Even Mengele's wife might have been a good mother. And probably Dr. Mengele was a good father. What does the son know about the mother he is born to or a mother about the child she gives birth to? Parents, like children, are accidental. The possible resemblances take root later. No one is born guilty of a guilt not his.

And if I was the daughter of Mengele? How would I have reacted as a grown-up to an executioner father I'd loved as a child, as an adolescent, and maybe even as an adult?

What should children of Mengele, of Hess, of Eichmann, do? I would not like to be in their place. I prefer mine. They too are branded, born to branders, whether they approve or disapprove of their parents. It's hard to carry a blame that's not yours.

No, no, don't worry, Mama, I'm not preoccupied with the children of the butchers, I'm not suffering for them, I don't go that far, but I don't envy them, as I don't envy the Germans in general. Though I know it's absurd, I often ask myself if it isn't nobler to be killed than to kill. You know what, Mama? It's crazy, I know, but I'm not normal; I'm content to be what I am. Seeing the worst has permitted me to understand people once and for all, the Jews too, Mama, we who after all we saw and suffered have got worse rather than better. Suffering doesn't ennoble people, Mama, not at all. Neither does faith— yours or the Christian's or Muslim's—I don't believe it. And don't tell me that I haven't understood anything, that I am a poor unfortunate stumbling in the dark, that life on earth means nothing, it's just a brief passage, an insignificant thing compared to eternity.

At this rate, you would have accepted even Auschwitz. Would have felt yourself chosen, honored by the most tremendous test that God could have inflicted on His people. Would have believed in Him in Auschwitz while they were incinerating your child or wife or sister. But really, Mama, you'll never never convince me that God wanted that. It's like saying that God is a monster, a Hitler.

"Bite your tongue," you used to say to me for much less, didn't you? "Die!" you'd say now if I let you, go ahead say it . . . I'm letting you speak. You're silent?

Or Papa might have had to throw you into the oven, or throw his children—the ones who never returned.

Would you have prayed as you threw me into the oven or would you have cursed the way Papa did when he couldn't endure life anymore. He would have had the courage even to say no, ready to die for us the way he was, as a young man, for our country, for you, Mama.

Do you remember that old song from the First World War that he sang for you in his beautiful voice?

In the documentary film that they made about me—I already mentioned it to you, didn't I?—I looked for the complete text. Now I have innumerable written versions and two tapes of the original; one is already worn out by too much use, the other is still new. Listen:

> I will never see you again, never never again
> and you won't see my tears for you.
> Uselessly I say your name,
> uselessly pour out my blood
> on the battlefield
> somewhere far from you.
> I am dying with no one to mourn me!
>
> Without even a fistful of earth
> on my abandoned grave,
> the bodies of the fallen will cushion me
> in the ditch where I'm thrown
> and no one will bend over my grave,

no one living,
nor will spring bring flowers.
The wind moves the faraway earth.

I wish that you could be mine one more time
cradling my nearly white head in your lap,
I wish I could consume myself on your lips,
live happy awake through the night.
Whatever else happens to me
I'll die in ecstasy for you
my wife, my country.

Do you remember? Papa sang it looking at you, trying to catch your eye that was always looking somewhere else. What is it you were refusing? His patriotism or his love?

"Poor idiot . . . ," you'd murmur every so often, shaking your head in Papa's direction. "He believes in his country . . . he wants to die for Hungary . . . When a Jew is an idiot he is too idiotic," you added in a monologue that luckily he couldn't hear, caught up as he was in the feelings that made his voice tremble.

You divided humanity into anti-Semite and not anti-Semite. The enemies of Hungary weren't your enemies, isn't that so?

"Look at the great Hungarian!" you complained every so often. "He wants to die for a country where when all's going well they barely tolerate you, look at you crooked, drive you away with a glance." So you admitted that someone could die and kill for his own country? If it had

71

been our country, our promised land, would you have looked lovingly at Papa? He sang so beautifully . . . Instead of listening when he sang not on a Jewish holiday for once, you made a wry face and commented scornfully, indignantly on this patriotic song invented by patriots for soldiers stuffed with patriotism.

Was it him you couldn't put up with anymore or the song? Though at one time I know that you loved each other very much, you married for love.

"It's impossible to love in poverty," you said, trying to defend yourself. "Poverty quarrels," you added, speaking in Yiddish to give a deeper truth, a tang, to the words.

In Yiddish a single word can express past, present, and future—one of your sighs was enough to tell the story.

When you said all of life was a tsoris, it wasn't just about the present, it was atemporal and included all time. It seemed as if that word came from time immemorial and would be true forever.

What a lovely language Yiddish was, Mama, a bastard language, expressive, rich and bittersweet as nostalgia. A beautiful language burned at Auschwitz along with those who spoke it: the grandfathers, the uncles, the aunts, you . . .

I haven't told you yet that Papa's older brother, the mythic David, that lucky, saintly man, as you used to say, who went to Palestine, I don't know how or when, died a few years ago in Scotland, having left the Promised Land to earn more money. The other brother, the youngest, is the only survivor among numerous brothers and sisters. I saw him after many years at Sara's house in Petah Tiqwa in Israel. He too lives in Scotland and goes to treat the infirmities of his old age at a place on the Dead Sea. You know, Mama, with us these relatives weren't either bad or good, just indifferent.

"It's your father's cursed family!" you repeat, and I tell you it was good to see him. He has Papa's skinny build, the same keen look, the same muteness—presence and absence at the same time.

I would not have said that wretched family knew how to cry, but, Mama, he cried!

He cried when Sara's little son, Ariel, as soon as he learned who his uncle was, ran and got the photo of Papa in uniform (that's the only one he has) and put it under his uncle's nose—that nose too small for a man. He burst into tears, maybe not just for Papa but for all the relatives, all the years, the children, life. It was the most beautiful thing he had ever done in our presence, his tears wiped out all my resentment, and while we ate next to each other, served by Golda, who was also visiting Sara, I looked at him for a long time, filled with an uncontainable feeling, I was trembling with the desire to embrace him, and I did it, I hugged him with the passion of a woman in love, shaken by sobs and pouring out tears I couldn't stop, into the soup, over the gnocchi, the chicken, the sweets, the coffee, frightening little Ariel who never heard of Auschwitz and is afraid in class when he hears the sirens sound.

"I'm no longer able to cry," Golda justifies herself, "I don't know how anymore," she says bitterly, almost as if she's angry at herself. With her heart guarded.

Ariel was clinging to his beloved mother's pants, between her legs, while she was asking her uncle questions about the past in her labored Hungarian. The child didn't understand our language or anything about us; his Germans are the Arabs; he covered his ears and hid his blond head in his mother's lap. "He understands, he understands . . . he hears," Sara told us while the dog arrived to console us all.

I would have liked to talk with my uncle, to complain about his parents, his spinster sisters, about my grandfather who didn't know which of his sons was my father or what my name was—but how could I? How can you speak ill of the dead and massacred? Of parents to their child?

My grandmother frightened me, with that face wrapped up in the kerchief tied under her chin, her face turned toward her prayer book, toward God, never deigning to give me a glance or a word, I won't say loving, but benevolent.

You were right, Mama. They didn't love us. Maybe they didn't know how to love. They weren't like your "robust family" with tender hearts.

Your mother was quarrelsome but she was there, she acted like a grandma; they were shut up in themselves, in their faith. Who knows what an awful childhood Papa had?

The only living uncle is seventy-three, Papa would have been ninety-three, like you. I love old people, Mama. Maybe I love them because of you. When I see a poor old man in some corner of the great city so unkind to the old, I think of you, of you both, knowing that if you were alive, Edy, Golda, and I would be parents to you.

I would have been a good mother to you, if you had survived as I did, maybe you would have been angry, maybe you wouldn't have talked to me anymore, would have denied me, continually asking yourself, asking me:

"But who are you? Where do you come from? How dare you do the things you do? How dare you say the things you say?"

I would answer you the way I always do, "I'm your daughter. I come from your belly."

You with your dissenting eyes would stare at your belly, and it would seem incredible to you that that belly could produce a girl like me, who has married a goy, who doesn't know how to pray, who has never been the way you wanted her to be and never will.

How many times you reproached me for having been born, just as I reproached you for bearing me. But I wouldn't do it anymore. I would let you talk, I would thank you. I do thank you. After all I am happy to live. Are you surprised? I'll never stop surprising you, will I?

"But what reason do you have to be content?" you would ask me even today. "You should be grateful to God, not to me," you would add, sighing a little toward heaven, and I'd start to smile like someone hiding a secret, an unmentionable mystery.

"She laughs, poor creature," I'd hear your resigned, pitying voice, disoriented by the world where, like my mother-in-law in her old age, you no longer feel at home. She too was lost when she confronted her daughter Nora—divorced like Sara with young children—she, who played Beethoven and translated Goethe, also had disagreements.

What difference is there then between cultures, between countries, between mothers, poor or bourgeois, between Christians, Jews, and nonbelievers?

Fundamental values and feelings are universal. The simple things that don't exist: justice, equality of spirit, the right to a dignified life for everyone. Everyone, Mama, without distinctions. Is that clear? That's my dream. An impossible dream of which I'm slightly embarrassed. It must sound like a cliché. But all simple things sound like clichés: faith, loyalty, love, piety, and truth. Truth! The only thing that sounds false.

You, who called Papa a liar, who made him seem like a man you couldn't trust and couldn't believe, you never understood anything. And how could you? What did you see or know besides your childhood home, which you left as a bride—your only dowry, your education, or rather the education of a poor Jewish girl from the country who awaited the Messiah, prayed, and hatched the children God wanted? Ten, twenty, thirty, what did it matter? It was God's will to bless or curse you with many children. *Abortion* and *divorce* weren't words you knew, they were blasphemous, shameful, mortal sins.

If you had lived, would I have divorced? Many more times. For the little I know myself, Mama, although I was a slavish daughter, I would have rebelled against your omnipotent will the way I did against your orders as a child.

"Go there, come here, bring me this, get me that, be quiet, don't talk to me, light the fire, get some water from the well, look for some kindling, run to the store for a little sugar on credit, don't ruin your shoes, be careful of your dress, pray, die, shut the door."

There it is, the things you said to me in our life together, and you said worse: "I'll break your neck, I'll beat you to a pulp, cut you to bits, I'll strangle you with my own hands, may I die if I don't kill you." Forgive me, Mama, if I remind you, I've forgiven you a long time ago. But as a little child I didn't understand forgiveness, I took refuge in poetry, under the bed, in the woods, far away from the meanness in your eyes, your curses, and your hands ready to strike.

"Sooner or later, you'll fall into my hands, you'll have to come out or go back home, if for no other reason than to fill your gut. If you don't want to die of hunger," you'd threaten. "If you only have a crumb of brain, I'll make you understand," you would shout after me. As I fled I'd ask myself, "But what does she want from me? What have I done? Why does she curse me? Why doesn't she love me? Why why why . . . It's not my fault that she is poor and irritable and tired."

It's not that I was afraid of you, Mama. I knew your rage would pass. At the worst you'd punish me by sending me to bed without supper, what a fuss over a cup of tea with saccharin and a piece of bread! Your words were what hurt me; I would have preferred a slap, a beating, or having my hair pulled. I even told you that, do you remember? No? I do. But I'm alive, how can I help remembering?

Calm down, I know you weren't a cruel mother, only poor and exasperated, but still I don't forget. What else can I remember about you? And what else could you do in your poverty?

What would I have done in your position? I don't know, Mama. We're so different, as if we weren't even relatives and didn't come from the same place.

I know impoverished mothers are harsher, even bad, they take out their helplessness on their children, on their husbands and neighbors, on anyone they see in their despair. A child of poverty grows up surrounded by yells, physical violence, a scarcity of love, but once grown up, he often defends himself better. He digs a place for himself in the world with his nails; he, who is nothing, wants to have something, be someone.

If I were crazier than I am, I would thank you for having brought me up in poverty. I'm stronger than the children of the rich; I survived even Auschwitz, where the bourgeois children fell first. But poverty still weighs on me, even today when I eat white bread. Someone who has been hungry never forgets hunger, just as the Jew can't forget that he is Jewish even when there is no longer an Auschwitz. To tell the truth, Mama, I don't know and I'll never know if you were a loving mother or not. Disinherited mothers have no possibility of expressing themselves, or of being something. This is the only thing that justifies you. If I didn't discuss things, how could I forgive you? Tell me. Speak to me! Say something—you who had an answer to every question. Your own. The only true and right answer drawn from the Bible.

Do you know what the Bible is today, Mama? Television! Images have taken the place of writing, of thought even. Images that cancel each other out up close and become confused, one with the other, images that at the same time mystify and demystify, consecrate and desecrate.

In your time it was easier to believe; today with the pope and the rabbi on television there is no more mystery, the pope is a man, like the rabbi—only the invisible attracts.

Technology is the real miracle; you can wash with a machine, Mama, ah, your hands always in water. Thinking is done by machine, and one can exterminate whole generations with a button. It's no longer necessary to soil your hands with blood or shoot from up close, or even look someone in the eye. One day people will be nostalgic for the beautifully human wars, hand-to-hand combat, army against army. Maybe as long as a man still sees his victim, there is some hope for a change of heart, a space for conscience, for memory.

How did you look at the man or woman who shoved you into the gas chamber?

If you looked at me, your daughter, with such a murderous gaze, you ought to have thundered against the enemy. Or at least awakened his conscience. Maybe there is a repentant Nazi around.

Though maybe, Mama, and this is what I believe, whoever kills dies a little, and the more he kills, the more he dies. Who knows how many dead men are walking the streets, particularly in Germany. Now they're old. They smoke pipes. They lie to themselves, to their children, to their grandchildren, to the world, they continue to lie in order to live, so they can stand the guilt.

They are unable to have one thought—clean, true— that isn't infected. Who knows how they really are? I ask myself how the murderer of ten thousand babies is doing.

I don't hate them, Mama. I don't know the feeling—it's rage that devours me, and impotence. I don't hate any-one but I'm afraid of everyone, that's true, above all I was afraid of you, then my superiors, the ones I depended on, the ones my work depended on.

Gabriele says that I'm strong, courageous even when I'm trembling inside, when I want to give up everything, even writing.

Don't shake your head commiserating with me, you ought to caress me to make me stronger.

Maybe even my body would be stronger if you had kissed me all over the way I've seen mothers do their naked babies after the bath. You didn't kiss my belly, my little feet, my sex, my bottom.

Did you ever caress me? I don't remember it, though I remember the precise faded color of your apron and the patches over the breast and the right pocket.

You must have kissed me when you left for Budapest but I only remember your return. I was dancing on the bed, and right away you got angry.

Even so, I know I was anything but a bad child, I just questioned things. You were the daughter, Mama, of a culture that thought it was enough to keep your children from starving.

If you could only see how Giorgio (Giorgio is my friend) loves his children, he thinks about them all the time, more than a motherly mother, he brings them my Hungarian salami, my Belgian chocolate, my Israeli pistachios—I anticipate his thought. He refers to them as children even though they are old enough to marry. For a psychoanalyst their relationship would be a gold mine, for me it's only beautiful. Tender. Constant. I too would have wanted a mama-father like this. But maybe his children don't, one never knows children's needs, we give them our needs, the way we do in love.

I have always felt a little like an orphan. Even when you were still with me. Papa had a thousand worries, you a thousand and one. You blamed Papa for everything except for not spending more time with us. When did a father ever talk or play with his child? You never played with us either. I know you didn't have the time, but couldn't you at least have given a gentle look, a smile, some sign of your presence—your love?

It's not that I want to reproach Papa for anything. You've already done it for all of us. You fought for us, attacked for us, in our name you asked everything from him, shoes, coats, bread, gloves, boots, grain, flour, potatoes, beans, schoolbooks. Maternal love often frightens me, and children are often vampires.

I bet that Mengele's mother also forgave her son. To a mother, her sons may be filth, commit crimes, steal, but they are still her children. But I, for a mere nothing, was no longer your daughter—for a little lie, a dirty word, a thought that differed from yours, my doubt in God. Because I laughed too much, cried for no reason. Because I broke the leg of an old chair.

You needed much less than that to push me away. To tell me that your belly had given birth to a stranger.

Several times I've seen your rejecting look in Edy's eyes—the eyes of Papa—when his only little boy has told a little lie. "Telling your father lies," Edy screamed, beside himself, lifting the child onto a stool as if he were a rabbit, to have him in reach. "I'll kill you," he babbled as if he'd gone mad. "Don't ever lie to me! I'm your father! I don't want a lying son! I'll kill you."

Little Shalom, who is always cheerful and smiling and happy to be in the world, looked at his father so stupefied that he didn't even cry despite repeated slaps.

He stood still with his eyes wide open after each slap, probably asking himself why. Why so much fury in such a good father who loves him so much. To him it seemed like a tremendous betrayal.

How could he know that in his father's rage there is the memory of a father who according to you, Mama, was a liar? The little innocent has paid for what happened to others, paid because his mama was in the hospital with lungs that had been bored through in Auschwitz, because life in the Promised Land promised so little to his father, nothing, and in fact he went away.

If you could see the world today, Mama, you'd prefer to be dead. But not even death has any value. Yesterday's dead haven't redeemed our right to be alive. Everything is the way it was before Auschwitz, with the difference that the martyrs of yesterday create their own martyrs.

And this is what I hate the most, Mama. Not even your martyrdom has served to make the world better or create a more just nation.

The museums to your memory are dead museums. There are too many dead to make a strong impression. Only in Jerusalem there is something chilling; a cold slab, endless, against the ground that was sown with the names of the Nazi Lagers, tongues of flame alongside them—an everlasting warning.

Israel ought to be the very memory of its people. Of the divine promise. If in the Diaspora we doubt, and talk about Auschwitz, and Israel becomes unworthy of your memory, if it disowns its submissive sons and wants them all stained heroes, then my letter too will be useless, the obsessions of a poor woman who insists that she and her people set an example.

But who is going to read tomorrow what they didn't read yesterday? Should perhaps the writer, who bears witness, commit suicide to give herself more readers? To better sell her work? Is it the best strategy for being more widely read, for making people remember, for surviving? Offering one's life for the sake of being remembered?

"Then I can kill myself too," beat inside my temples while Giorgio was telling me about my writer friend's suicide.[1]

"He killed himself," repeated Giorgio on the phone. "He killed himself," he confirmed while the mouthful I was eating stuck in my throat.

"It's impossible, it's absurd." I attacked Giorgio as if he himself had pushed him to suicide. "What are you saying? I don't believe it." Had he dared? I asked myself, as frightened as if I were alone in the world, as if I were his daughter, betrayed and abandoned.

"I'm not going to write anymore either," I said to myself. He was the rallying point, the force of testimony; what use was I now? Since neither he nor anyone else will ever be able to say what a survivor is and what it is that he has survived and what makes a survivor kill himself.

---

[1] The writer friend is Primo Levi, who died in 1987.

Here, now, in a letter to you, is the last time I will speak of it. Let me talk one last time; I want to speak, just like the dying man who wants to smoke his last cigarette. Pressing my memory for what hasn't yet been said. The memories of you, of us, can't be dispersed, otherwise I'm lost and I lose you.

Maybe my letter to you is only an instrument for writing about Auschwitz, but you and Auschwitz are inseparable, like Dachau and Papa. He stayed there, did you know that he died of exhaustion and hunger? He let himself die, the coward.

Oh, how I wished that he'd come back. I would have dressed him in gold, made him a monument, overwhelmed him with love, kept him chained to my side . . .

Are you jealous? He would finally have been mine. Unlike you, he would have lived with me; he even ate pork.

"Pork," I hear you say. You still judge people by what they eat.

The last time I ate pork, I was at Dachau. Yes, Dachau, Mama, a small, ancient town, renowned for the first German concentration camp, where today there is a museum instead of the camp that more and more resembles a nursery school, where in an alehouse I asked an old citizen the whereabouts of the museum.

"I don't know," he answered, shaking his head, swallowing beer, and looking at me as if I'd asked to go to the moon.

"You don't know . . ." came from my mouth already full of bile, because the camp-museum was only a few steps away.

"No," he repeated with an innocent look, offended by my expression, which was more than incredulous, annihilated. I went back to my seat, repeating to myself that I knew it, knew that he would answer that way—why had I wanted to talk to him? Why had I given in to the temptation of interrogating him?

I tell you, you are blessed, Mama, I too would have rather died before they cast doubt on the gas chambers, before that German in 1988 shook his head, before I read on the walls of Rome, "Death to the Jews."

"Don't torment yourself," you say?

Yes, I torment myself. And I write. I write to you because you are my mother. I could also have turned to Papa but I confess it never occurred to me. I don't believe he would have had the patience to listen to me, sometimes he didn't even seem to know my name. He didn't fight with me the way you did. He never said anything to me. He didn't talk. He was mute. Impotent. He didn't even chat with God, the way you did. He was alone. He didn't speak to anyone. He was the most solitary man I ever knew.

When I jumped on him, when I began to kiss him, to torment him with my attacks of love, for once you rose up in his defense: "Leave him in peace! Let him rest. Don't annoy your father. Get down from there!" you ordered if I sat on his lap, his bones grating against mine.

"No," I'd answer, searching in his pockets full of nothing, of tobacco strands, of dust.

Then you'd come to take me and drag me away. I'd hang on to his skinny neck, kissing his head that smelled of refried oil.

You were jealous, weren't you? You were right. I loved him so much. When I grew up, I would have married him. I always spied on him when he was taking off his shirt, his pants. When he washed his hairy armpits, opened his mouth to yawn, shaved himself in front of the mirror.

I like Edy because he resembles him. Edy's son too, because all three resemble each other. I even liked my uncle a little, I confess. I confess everything because there is nothing to confess.

There is only one thing I haven't told you yet. I also worked as a dancer. In a troupe of immigrant orphans who were looking for a place to live after Auschwitz.

Don't yell, don't yell. I didn't enjoy myself. Listen before you condemn me. Let me talk. Then say whatever you want. Just the way Edy and Golda did. Say your worst, but let me talk. Don't act the all-powerful. The righteous. The dictator. Listen: I didn't know what to do with myself in a world without a place for the survivors. Not even in Israel. Don't look incredulous, it's not an accusation to justify my errors. When I entered the country, it was newborn. Three months old. A baby in need of everything and everyone, like us survivors, naked, longing for love, for constant protection, sweet words, understanding, open arms, balm for the wounded soul.

The little country at war, always at war from the moment it came into being, ought to be populated by loving mothers, by psychoanalysts, not by armed soldiers. And it ought to be running with milk and honey as it did in your stories, not with more blood, theirs and others, shed by their hands. As soon as I arrived, the army swallowed my husband of two days instead of welcoming us with some kind words, hot tea. With a smile. A friendly explanation, in a family spirit. Why so much hurry to separate us as soon as we set foot on the earth dreamed about for a lifetime, for all the lifetimes of the Jews?

I don't want to tell you about the entrance camp where I waited for a place to live, to work, to exist. I won't tell you about the barracks of red-hot sheet metal or of the interminable lines for food, or the fights between the thirty cohabitants, men and women together, Mama.

My weakness of having my feelings immediately hurt, being humiliated, was your fault, it was you who deluded me, who guaranteed happiness and friendly support to anyone who crossed the sacred threshold. Even though I doubted the existence of your God's goodness, deep inside I believed in your stories, until reality—which I can't stand even today—gave you the lie. I feel Israel in my flesh, in my blood, in my spirit that revolts against every injustice that it commits.

How could I not believe you, Mama? You were my mother. With only one word, only a glance you cured my appendix, my headache, my freezing feet. One smile from you, never like the one in the photograph, cleared the clouds from the sky. If you were aware of me, it was enough to keep me from being jealous of your God to whom you were totally devoted; you spoke more to that One in a day than you did to me in all my life.

But our time together was too short, Mama, and so full of miserable necessities that it left you no time for us.

I went to school hurriedly drinking a tea with saccharin—you were already suffering because there was no sugar, bread was scarce, and you didn't know what you were going to cook for lunch or dinner.

I wouldn't want to get up because it was cold enough to make my teeth chatter, and I'd begin to complain about my things. What would I wear to go out? What firewood could I take to school if we didn't have any ourselves? What could I take for a snack? Only bread? Always bread when the other children had something inside it. I'm sorry, Mama, I shouldn't have done that, I knew very well that you couldn't do anything, but I too had reason to complain, I was ashamed to go to school without wood. Being Jewish was already a fault; poverty redoubled the contempt.

"Don't torture me, don't say a word," sometimes you said, shutting my mouth before I opened it. I complained all the same, but at least we talked, we fought and you hit me. "Eat me," you would say every once in a while, opening your arms wide in a heroic gesture. "Here I am," you would say and stop in the middle of the kitchen dark as a cell.

I would look at you amused by the idea of eating you, of giving you a good bite, but then I realized that I would hurt you and I already felt bad for you, I almost started to cry, telling you that I would never eat you not even if I were starving, I would leave you the way you were, beautifully round, plump with velvety skin and heavy thighs. You were complete this way, perfect, with arms just right for you, strong flanks, a face round and rosy like a mama-doll. A doll ready to sacrifice, first for God and then for her children.

Would you have let yourself be eaten? Did you act the heroine because you weren't risking anything and it shut us up immediately? Rather, it made us feel guilty because we had exasperated you—us, always us.

If you didn't say, "Here I am, eat me," you would suggest that we pray for bread, for wood, for clothes, to drive way our enemies, to live in peace, to go, as quickly as possible, to Palestine.

How many prayers never said, Mama.

"And you even boast of it . . ." You want to say that, don't you? But I'm not boasting about anything, I'm not making fun of faith. I believe, Mama. No no don't shout with joy, I don't believe in prayer, or the candle lit on Friday night, or the fast on Yom Kippur, I believe in the honesty of my civil conscience. You don't know what that is; rest easy, I'm a good Jew.

"That's what you say," you insist in your profoundly stubborn ignorance. Mama, I didn't mean, don't intend, to offend you. I only want you to understand me enough to realize that I've given you more than a prayer.

"Not even a Kaddish?" you complain.

Yes, maybe you're right, but saying Kaddish didn't feel sincere. In my work, I can't do what doesn't feel sincere, so how could I with the faith that was everything to you? You had a secure refuge while Papa buried his head in his hands, and if you had not goaded him into movement the way you would a tired horse, he would never have moved from the chair where he collapsed exhausted and hopeless. I understood him. I too have moments in which I want to stop and say, "Enough," and still you are there, your memory, to spur me to continue, to talk about you and remember you.

"Who knows when he'll come back?" you asked your-self and us when Papa closed the door, disappearing without even a farewell. And the wait began. For you, it was filled with sighs, for us with dreams, candies, boots, shoes, clothes, a ball promised a million times, a father who was slow to return.

Every time he came back, he was the Messiah, even if his hands were empty, he had returned, returned!

"Thank God, safe and sound," you added.

For the poor everything was supernatural, doubly so for the Jew.

While you finished your prayer, I asked Papa where he'd been for so long, where he'd slept and eaten, who he'd seen, what the world was like.

I did it for your sake too, Mama, I preceded you in jealous interrogation. Yes, Mama, you were jealous and suspicious, you were afraid of betrayal.

"How can I trust someone like you," you'd say to him. "A Jew that acts like a goy!"

Poor man, if I think about it, Mama, I think he was a faithful husband. For no other reason than because he was a man and nothing more, because of how he was raised, like your son, Edy. He too is a faithful husband.

Were you and Papa happy once? Before all of us were born?

Mama, I can be happy over nothing, over a piece of crusty bread, another gold ring, when I write. Sometimes happiness enters me without any reason, sometimes when I am most alone. In a solitary afternoon a black wave invades me, when it seems that I have everything, no urgent wants or lacks, then like my writer friend who killed himself I think there is no hope, there has never been and never will be.

"There is no more hope," my writer friend told me on the phone. Coming from his mouth, it seemed true to me. "It was better in Auschwitz," he added, and it seemed to me that he was swearing. "At least then I was young and I believed, you understand?" He bit off the phrases that must have disturbed him too.

I disagreed but in silence, struck dumb by what I heard, but he was listening only to himself anyway, convincing himself that he couldn't write anymore, that he had no more to say, even his English had left him, all he could do now was stay by the side of his blind and sick mother to note down her sensations.

"Do you realize?" he concluded in a hurry. "I don't know if I'll write another book."

"Certainly you'll do it, and you'll write many others besides." I consoled him as you console intelligent children who know everything, who know that words have their content and that what you say happens.

I never dreamed that in a short while, a few days before Passover, he would fly from the third floor after talking with the concierge, who called him professor and brought him letters from so many people.

But who could have believed that suddenly, with no one being aware of anything—his beloved sister, his wife, his sons, his friends—he would fly like a tired angel when faced with that fatal moment that overcame reason in a reasonable man.

What phantom was he fleeing? Did he think he could survive once again? But he did survive. He succeeded. He's alive. I've never thought of him as dead. When I say his name, it's the name of someone alive, and his books are more alive than ever. It is only when I look at one of the many photographs of him alive that I see he is dead.

The last time I saw him alive, he was just the same, alert, tense as a human guinea pig, watchful inside and out. He walked with short cautious steps, without making too much noise, putting his feet down as if he were sneaking, moving forward without haste but with an internal urgency, like someone who hasn't managed to finish something or isn't sure that he'll have time to finish. He was always amazed, almost as if he didn't live in the world; he looked at everything as if it were for the first time, like a child who discovers things, or a convalescent who emerges from years of sickness.

In Rome he felt like an outsider, being from Turin, a city with a colder spirit, more aristocratic. The Roman sun and Roman colors dazzled his keen eyes, which were half closed in front of the windows sparkling as if it were Christmas. "So many beautiful things," he'd say. It seemed as though he had never seen such riches, even though he'd lived in a richer city than Rome.

"What wonderful sun," he added, looking at me as if I'd given him the sun or he himself had invented it.

"Why don't you come to Rome for a while?" I asked him, often.

"To Rome?" he asked the way someone would ask, "Where's Rome?"

"Yes, yes, to Rome." I tried to convince him. Again, the last time we talked on the telephone.

"I'm so depressed." He abandoned himself to his melancholy.

"Rome is good for people who are depressed," I joked stupidly, then even more stupidly I told him a series of banalities.

"We can't give in. We can't. Living is a duty for us, we ought to live forever, be immortal, isn't it so, aren't we immortal and indestructible?

On the other side of the line he must have smiled his bittersweet smile, staying there suspended in silence, alarming, cold, impatient.

"I so much want to see you," I said, trying to excuse myself for reminding him of our duty that he understood only too well. He had lived in that duty with a mind always alert to what was happening in the world. Did he want to free himself, with his suicide, from these very obligations? What did he want to free himself from? Why?

A person so fine, Mama, at times he seemed so stunned, so ingenuous, so humble, so surprised by his success that I asked myself whether he was really like that or just acting modest.

He was a man that people esteemed, loved, listened to, read. He had enough to eat, to cover himself, a nice house that he owned, a family where he was a prophet—perhaps not listened to—a country, Italy, that he felt belonged to him, an Italian Jew.

"What more did he want?" you ask, judging him ungrateful, a person who only needed to thank God. But he too was an unbeliever, Mama, even if, in my opinion, atheists are the most religious. Like my mother-in-law, like Gabriele and all the atheists surrounding me. And none of them are afraid of God or the Last Judgment.

You, on the other hand, feared Him so much, you were terrorized by Him, by His punishments, His displeasure, His oversights, His disaffection, you spent your life trying to please the Invisible One, fleeing what you saw.

I, unlike you, Mama, don't fear God, only human beings. Why should He punish me?

I hear your eloquent breathing, the same way you were breathing when you sewed the star of yellow fabric on my breast.

Your breath was dense, hot, near my tense face, almost proud as if you were decorating me, because I'd been good. You were bowed at my feet, you sighed, pricked me, pricked yourself. "Don't move," you rebuked me, who did not move, at attention like a soldier.

"Stay still, stay still!" you scolded me at intervals. Instead of crying I started to laugh, saying that I liked the star; that now I was myself, no one would say to me anymore that I didn't seem Jewish. No one would have any doubts as to what I was. I was legitimate.

Reinforced by that distinction, I watched with pleasure as you cut stars for all the family from a rag you had dyed yellow. You were rapt, engaged, concentrated, a child playing tailor for her doll. Were you playing? You were so precise, good, able, unlike me, who didn't know how to trim, design, or embroider.

Your stars all came out perfect, like your children, with six identical points, the cuts all equal, not like the blouse for my rag doll. Congratulations! Well done!

"My star is prettier," I teased Golda who got as angry as if I'd said, "I'm the prettier one."

Golda scolds me even now for having said certain things, for having been a child full of myself, who got spoiled by myself, was predicted a great future, disdained housework, saying that I would do great things, something other than washing the plates and being a servant all my life to my husband and children.

From the way I was, Mama, not even I would have guessed that I would have become a good cook, a good wife, a maniacal prisoner of my house, rented by me for who knows how much longer. And I'm also a hard worker. You don't believe it, do you? I don't pass a day without working. I work on Saturdays, Sunday, Passover. If I don't do something useful, I feel useless. At a certain age perhaps, we are children of ourselves, of our neuroses?

If this is how it is, you aren't much of a mother to me these days, that's why I'm writing you, to make myself known, but I will always be your daughter. It's you who ought to read me, even if no one else ever does.

"Write write write," you say, unable to take any more of my writing. "Nice thing, nice profession, to spread on the four winds what ought to be kept in the family, between four walls. Couldn't you have done some honest, real work, the proper kind? Do you need to see your name everywhere? You always wanted to stand out. Haven't they singled you out enough? Wasn't that enough for you? You're vain, you always wanted something special, you tormented me for a hair ribbon, for a new hairstyle, for a lace collar like the one worn by the teacher's daughter, for black patent-leather shoes! You weren't satisfied the way Golda was, you always wanted to be a proper little lady, you read poetry instead of praying." You reiterate the great sins of my childhood, which I no longer commit as an adult, even though I still love ribbons, lace, poetry, the things I have around me, my house that isn't mine but that I'm as afraid of losing as I am of losing myself, and you who are looking at me from every corner, I know, even in the dark, the place where your picture is hanging on the wall. At night when I wake suddenly, I'm aware of every object and corner edge just as if it were full daylight. I know the story of each thing, its price, just when it came into my possession. This house is my history. My country. My family.

I don't like things that are new, new clothes, new shoes, unknown streets, a new dentist, novelty, fashion. I wear the same dresses for ten or twenty years, just like you.

I bring them out every winter and they are familiar to me, and I to them, they always suit me, I know where I bought them, on what occasion, they tell me everything, they know about me, they make me remember myself, they have their own memories, their own voice.

Throwing away an old dress because of some wrinkles is like doing plastic surgery on your memory, canceling your past, the signs of life.

Unlike most men and women, I love wrinkles, Mama. What kind of a face is a face without signs, without something written, incised on it? It's like not having a face, not having a past.

If you hadn't had that deep crease around your mouth, I wouldn't still remember your mouth, or your nose above the mouth, or your watchful eyes.

If you hadn't always worn the same dress with the white lace collar for all the ceremonies, happy or funereal, I wouldn't remember your large body to which I would have liked to return.

I want my wrinkles. I don't even use makeup. I look like a sick person in this highly colored, perpetually shining world, where everyone wants to be beautiful, to be instantly striking, to put on a dazzling show.

Mama, remember how much I liked crazy people and funerals? I still do. Even today I follow casual funeral processions, I stop to look at crazy people, people on the margins, those who are outside life.

Those who once were tied up in the cellar like our poor Irma.

Today I saw one on the sidewalk of a wide Roman street. He seemed like a rag. A heap of scraps from a secondhand market. A circus animal or a great dead bird. On the dark ground of his coat he had attached colored strips like feathers, around his neck hung two old bicycle wheels and a flaccid tire, his feet were bound into furry paws with sharpened nails. His bearded face was half hidden by a wide brimmed hat full of holes. He seemed young, Mama, and very handsome with alert, hazel eyes. It was terrible to see him, Mama, because he was fully aware of himself and of the others.

People surprised and a little frightened by that presence forgot to throw him something, and I felt ashamed, I don't know why.

I would have liked to speak to him, to sit down next to him. When I was little I always slipped away to go to Irma. I listened carefully to what she said to me, as if she might reveal some mystery, that extra something that the insane know but the normal don't, something similar to what the pope, the grand rabbi, or a guru might tell me.

Our poor crazy one didn't know how to talk, only to swear, to say bad words, shout, shut herself in an incredible silence, shake the chains that bound her, pick up food spilled on the ground amid the excrement.

And sometimes she cried, Mama; no one went to see her besides me. I listened awaiting the word, I laughed when she laughed, sang with her if she sang, but we didn't swear, that we wouldn't do, we cried together.

"You're not normal," you protested, "going to see that lunatic, you can't be normal."

You never called her by name. For you and the others she was simply the lunatic, just as we Jews were only Jews and the Gypsies were only Gypsies. The oppressed, the minorities, those who are different, quickly lose their names; rather, they don't have names, they are named by group, and naming one, you name them all. The lunatics, the pederasts, the Jews, the blacks, the Gypsies . . . then you wonder why children grow up racist.

"I don't understand you, I'm not listening to you anymore, what do you want from me, I didn't even know what that crazy woman was called," you defend yourself. You knew, I told you, but you didn't hear me, you had no ears for me, for you everything was more important than I was: the potatoes to peel, stockings to mend, blowing on the fire I was supposed to make though I hadn't found a single dry piece of wood in the forest. And how could I, Mama, in January?

If you had listened to me once to the end, maybe I wouldn't be writing you now, maybe I would never have written a book. I owe this, my writing sickness, to you, and to Auschwitz where you let go of me, rather pushed me away, screaming at me to obey the man who was beating me with his gun.

I already wrote you a few lines in one of my previous books, then discouraged, I put away the idea.

What was there to talk to you about? I didn't know. And I don't know even now, I haven't planned either the content or the end or anything else, I'm moving blindly, I say anything to you just to keep you, waiting for the end to arrive on its own, and then I'll let you go, I'll let you rest in peace and I'll be at peace with you and you with me.

"To rest in peace with a daughter like you who hasn't said a prayer for her mama, not one Kaddish!" you say, blackmailing me.

Let's forgive each other, Mama. I'm your daughter. You're my mother. I love you because you're my mother and you love me because I'm your child. If I had been the daughter of another mother, I would love another mother; instead, you are the only one for me, like your God, ours, if there is one.

I don't accept your death, and because of that, I'm unacceptable to you.

When my mother-in-law died, in her white bed, at eighty-four, I cried, yes, but I didn't rebel against God, as you would say, or the law of nature, it was right that she died, she had lived and grown old, she had ended her natural cycle, she said so herself, calmly, with the serene rationality of a layperson, a naturalist, a puritan goddess.

If you had died the way she did, with your children around you, sooner or later I would have been at peace as all children are. I would have accepted that you were gone, you had been old, and old age means death. If you had lived the life you were destined to live, my soliloquy would have been unnecessary, sooner or later we would have talked, I don't say we would have understood each other, perhaps this would never have happened, oh, what pain I would still have to put up with, I would have done everything to make you appreciate me for who I am.

You don't understand that I am trying to get your approval, your blessing. If you want me to pray, I will, but don't ask me to swear that I believe, I don't like to promise, I'm always afraid I won't be able to keep my word. I can't lie about faith, Mama. I'm too religious.

You smile? Who knows, maybe if you'd prayed less, if you'd believed less, if men with faith hadn't been so evil, I would be a believer.

"Stop praying!" I often annoyed you by saying, when I saw you blindly praying over your book. "I want to tell you something," something more important to me as a child, but you pushed me away with an eloquent moan, forgot about me, you didn't care anything about anyone, you were elsewhere with God, the house might even burn down, I might die! When you finished praying, you might even punish me.

"What good did it do you to pray?" I asked you, moving away with a lump in my throat that didn't go away even when I cried.

"Cry! You dare to cry. Idiot! First, you don't let me pray in peace and then you cry for nothing. Listen to her. She acts as if someone were skinning her. Be quiet! Stop it! The crown has fallen from her head. She's offended. Suffers! But what's wrong? Why are you crying? Eat. That's enough already!"

"I don't want anything," I shouted.

"All the better. There'll be more left over. Starve if you want, but stop crying, explain yourself!"

How could I tell you why I was crying? After all, you hadn't really done anything to me. How could I have told you about that sensation of universal unlove that my friend, the writer who committed suicide, must have felt too.

These are such solitary sensations, apparently irrational but connected to the most profound reality. There is a sort of vertigo of reason, a great cold, a black lucidity.

You know, Mama, I believe in destiny but I don't yet understand by what criteria it is distributed and by whom.

Certainly it's not by a rational, just, reasonable, being, it all seems senseless, a contagious chaos. If it's all in God's hands, either He doesn't know what He is doing or I haven't understood anything, give too much importance to life on earth, am without a soul.

"Do you enjoy tormenting me?"

You smile. You stare. You listen to me as if you want to know where this is going to end.

I don't know but I wish you'd listen to me attentively, without acting like a mother. Be a friend. Pretend that we have been friends since I became your daughter and you my mother.

There, when I think that you're my friend I already feel freer, I fear you less and I can tell you more about myself. What I hide when I'm writing, what's between the lines, behind the words, the self-censuring.

Remember when I told you that I'd written a poem for you that you didn't bother to read or even listen to, when I read it aloud? It was a day in April. There was a cold sun, and a stiff wind whirled about in the courtyard where you had started a fire to make us popcorn. Popcorn, Mama, that's how you say it now, in the American way, not maize.

The popping seeds flew like white butterflies crazed by coming into the world. You were beautiful. With your rosy cheeks. Your dark hair coming out of the kerchief that had slipped back on your head, giving you a much less severe, almost frivolous air, as if you were glad to give birth to those flakes for us, which we ran after over-joyed, as if they were manna from heaven.

In that moment I understood that God is a woman—not a man—a little like you, creatress of my every good and evil. I wrote something like that in my first poem, and this is what I've tried to say as an adult. That you were a magician, a witch, the white and black, yes and no, happiness and pain. I wanted it to be written somewhere what your arms were like, your gestures as you peeled potatoes, washed clothes, kneaded bread. Under your hands, even the water became sweet, the holes vanished, the chickens were plucked, the duck grew heavier, the chair no longer wobbled.

How could I possibly forget you or let you be forgotten? If you want to know, you have become more alive for me since you died. As long as you existed, it was natural that you were there. In the Lager, hunger canceled memory, fear devoured all my energy, all my attention. Only once in a while, when someone was observing the holidays, you would come to my mind along with the whole house, the chickens, the courtyard, the kitchen, the down comforter, and all the weight of your unbearable absence.

I cursed the holiday, the one who had remembered, the one who prayed, who cried for his relatives, who sang in Yiddish in the dark.

Even now, I try to forget the holidays, along with the television and the newspapers that announce Yom Kippur and the anniversary of the Yom Kippur War in Israel. They were shooting even on Yom Kippur, in Israel. They were shooting on Yom Kippur, Mama, and you scolded me for so much less, for a symbolic, purifying act. And what if I'd been in Israel and had been shooting like so many women, what would you have said? Which is the worse sin, to kill or, remembering hunger, to eat something when it's there and thank God as you said, because not everyone in this world has something to eat?

You can't stand any more of me, can you? Because I speak a little like you, it seems as if I have an answer for everything and it's no less true than yours. Truth is more than a mama, it's infinite, everyone possesses a pinch of it, maybe all the truths together make up God. Isn't it parceled out to each of us, even the worst of people?

Don't congratulate yourself, I'm not going your way, and if we meet in some afterlife, our ways will be different, even if I reach you, or you me.

For me to hear you, all I have to do is cook something that you cooked, I cook it and eat it with boundless appetite, as if I were eating your body.

To feel your punishment, all I have to do is eat a pork chop and you make me throw it up, make me die of stomachache.

Can it be possible that you'll watch me forever, forbid me everything? You make me blush for a childish lie, you make me tremble in front of whoever sits behind a desk, bow my head when I should be lifting it, you inject me with fear, with excessive humility, as if I owed everything to everyone, as if I were alive only through grace.

"A Jew ought to be thankful every day," you often repeated, then one day you were speaking Yiddish, the secret language that you used with Papa at important times, to talk about terrible things, pogroms here, pogroms there, and I understood that the Jews had been drowned in the Dnieper—which could only have been a river, a Russian river that I'd learned about in school from my geography teacher.

I will never ever be able to eat a good ham without your looking into my mouth.

It's a shame that you don't understand the love of animals, Mama, their grace, their animal fidelity.

You only know the flesh of animals, and not even much about that. You touched them only to fatten them, weigh them, feel their livers, the fat, the egg in the behind, the feathers for the cushion. Already, while they were still alive, you divided their flesh into portions, their fat, perhaps enough to cook with from Channukah to Passover. You know, Mama, when I was little I felt sorry for the animals as well as for the lunatics. Either they were eaten, or driven away with sticks, or treated cruelly.

I've had birds, dogs, cats, and if it was possible, I would have lived in a zoo.

I found my first white dog on the streets of Tel Aviv, and we became two wanderers.

The second puppy was given me by a drunken American sailor in a bar in the port of Piraeus.

The third, a wolf, I found among the Roman garbage heaps and after eight months of care, he died in one of those hospices for dogs where, as in the Lager, only the strongest survive.

Don't undervalue my love for and attraction to animals, to the mad and to funerals; animals are mysterious, lunatics too, and like the dead: they know something that we don't, that we are trying to understand, imagine, interpret.

The puppy given to me by the Piraean sailor was still blind, he drank from a bottle and grew in my lap when we were together, when he wasn't alone crying while he waited for me as I was trying to tell my right leg from my left and to raise it in time with the others, trying to lift my arm with a touch of grace without bumping the musicians, who like me were survivors of Auschwitz, adrift in the world.

"Damn, oh God, do it over," they despaired in Yiddish, throwing me baleful looks that confused me even more at the finale when I had to do a back bend without breaking myself in two.

I did my best, Mama, and after a while I was good, I was a soloist in Athens and Istanbul, where I fell in love with the landlord's father, who was dying of cancer. His serene smile seemed like a miracle with all those tubes in his body, the plastic sacks hanging by the side of the bed.

He took my hand, I took his, and, not being able to talk, not having a common language, we limited ourselves to looking at each other, and making signs like deaf-mutes without ever misunderstanding each other. He had white hair, longish and yellowed here and there; his handsome face was hollowed out, like the dying, all eyes. But his glance didn't frighten me, and I wasn't afraid of catching his mortal illness. I believe he was the first old man that I ever loved in place of Papa, who wasn't old. You seemed older to me even though you were the same age. Papa didn't give birth to us the way you did! He didn't even behave like a father to us.

Do you remember my acrobatics on the bed? In the courtyard, in the middle of the kitchen? You said I seemed made of rubber. At home I never bumped into anything with my back bends and contortions, but on the stage I immediately became disoriented, the way I usually am in cities, in the world.

I often get lost in Rome. Then I stop. I try to figure out where I am. What the streets are called. Where they begin and where they end. I know ahead of time that I'll be confused, go the wrong way, and as if I were a stranger, I ask where my street is, my neighborhood, my country.

Telling you about my life as a dancer won't just scandalize you, it will hurt you, make you unhappy. If I hadn't been twenty years old with my whole life ahead of me to live, to prove myself, I would have said, "Enough." But there was time to repair, to hope . . . there was the future, everything was possible.

"Enough"—are you telling me that, too?

I'm not finished and you haven't made peace with me. You're resisting. As with Papa, whom you never forgave, as if poverty were a crime. You held up your brothers, more gifted at business, as examples, especially your favorite, Miki. You know what Miki did? One of those nights when my uncles, who were traveling for business, had to sleep with us, he touched me with his fat ugly dirty hands between my legs that were rigid with terror. Yes, Mama, yes!

He pretended to sleep, my uncle who smelled of sweat, of stall hay, of filth. Forgive me. I oughtn't. The martyrs of Auschwitz are sacred. But you didn't let me sleep with Papa, I slept with your brother whom you valued more than Papa.

And if I'd told you then about my first wakeful night, of fear and helplessness, knowing that it would be useless to denounce your brother, you wouldn't have believed me. "Crazy liar!" you would have yelled. "Disappear from my sight, whore, to say something like that about my brother Miki! Miki the good, the gentlest, the most unlucky because of his viper of a wife, the most pious, he always wears his yarmulke (not like that goy your father), takes good care of his family, has two horses, a gig. With his wife at the store—even if no one came to it because Rifka was ugly as sin.

How could I have defended myself against your absolute truth? I really felt sorry for myself, I felt alone.

"You're having your revenge because this one time he didn't bring you candy? Eh?" you would have hurled another accusation, seeing me solitary, thoughtful, too serious not to worry you.

"You were angry because I gave him two eggs at dinner!" From then on you would never have stopped provoking, guessing, unbosoming yourself in order to put any suspicion at a distance. "The one time my brother comes to dinner, my children act like Gypsies, they look into his mouth, steal mouthfuls with their glances. My children have no dignity, they have to let everyone know that they're always hungry. Then he goes home and tells everything to that witch of a wife, who never sent us a single hen though she has more than a hundred. May she and her hens all die." You might have concluded with that, or you might have continued speaking of your troubles, you wouldn't have stopped, maybe you would even cry to increase my suffering.

You are silent. You don't know what to say. What to think. I've troubled you. You begin to soften, just as you continued reproving Papa in an almost pacifying tone, continued to suspect him but without conviction.

"Look what a state you're in," you said after his return from a trip to get bread. "What will you wear on Yom Kippur? You've ruined your good suit, wasn't your everyday one good enough for sleeping in the stalls with cow dung and horseshit? Take your jacket off and I'll fix it for you, you don't have a human face anymore! It's covered with dirty straw. Oh, there's a blond hair! Where did you sleep? With whom? How disgusting. Tell me."

"I haven't done anything, I didn't sleep with anyone," my father babbled. "Maybe it stuck to me on the train."

"What train? Didn't you leave with your bicycle? Where is your bicycle?"

"Yes, with the bicycle, maybe the wind brought the hair to me, at the market."

"Where is the bicycle?"

"They stole it from me," he blurted out.

"Stole! You sold it for beer!"

"Yankel is my witness, he was there when it happened."

"Yankel, that good-for-nothing. Not even married. Do you expect me to trust a Jew like him who goes with shiksas?" You became more indignant with Yankel than with Papa, and I defended him, saying that maybe he was so happy, nice, always smiling because he didn't have a wife and children to support.

"You be quiet." You turned to me, extending your arm and opening your hand to block my view.

Papa, despoiled of everything to be mended, wrapped up in a blanket, became ever smaller, ever more hidden. He was asleep or pretending to sleep, like Uncle Miki, and you lowered your voice even though you continued to suspect Papa, as you washed, brushed, disinfected his clothes.

"Would Papa be happy too, if he weren't married?" I asked you and you didn't know whether to laugh or cry.

"If he weren't married, you wouldn't be here and I wouldn't have to be the mother of a daughter like you," you answered.

"What am I like?" I asked, seeing you disposed to talk to me.

"How do I know? Only God knows. A person no longer knows her own children, her husband, her relatives, or neighbors, no one!" you say. "Only God can know everyone and everything," you tell me as if warning me to be as good as I can because Someone notices me, knows everything I do. You could tell me anything you wanted, it was enough that you talked to me, that you didn't get too angry at Papa, of whom you were as jealous as I was of Gabriele when I went to spy on him. Unlike Papa, Gabriele was guilty. Nevertheless that evening he held his head high, drank, toasted, talked, and was satisfied.

Are you crying, Mama? No. If you like, I won't speak of Papa anymore. I'll remind you only of me, of us two. Maybe my memories are exaggerated, invented, distorted the way Edy and Golda say. In truth Edy has never read one of my books. Golda discouraged it. Only once did I read Edy a poem of mine translated into Hungarian and dedicated to Papa.

116

It was the first real poem I'd written. Maybe the most beautiful. Edy listened to me impatiently, pacing like a prisoner between the sofa and the breakfront full of his porcelain horses and his wife's crystal.

At the end, I read:

> Take me father
> I'll give you pleasure not children
> love not duty
> love not reproaches
> love unknown to you
> imagined by me, run
> it's the time of the Apocalypse
> let's commit a mortal sin
> to deserve death.

He turned his back and didn't turn to me again or say one word; he went to the kitchen and asked for dinner in an impatient voice.

But if I wrote what was false, I'd do it wholeheartedly, just as when you prayed, you forgot everything else.

I too am elsewhere when I write; just as you were with God, I am with you and drive away even the cats, putting away even friends, the people dearest to me; I forget to eat, to drink, to telephone, to have backaches.

I wish I'd invented it all, I wish you'd died in your own bed.

"Auschwitz," you pronounce slowly as if it were the sacred name of God, the most sacred unpronounceable place on the earth. Instead we should all talk about it. There should be an obligatory school to teach it.

What were our last years at home but the antechamber to Auschwitz? A little bit more fascist propaganda, a bit of scorn from the church, and no one would have saved that poor old man Roth attacked on the way back from the synagogue by boys who a little while before had been nice, just like the others, neither friends or enemies.

"Worm, your time has come," they said to him, throwing him in the muddy water alongside the street. "If I like, I'll squash you like a flea. Drown you. Bust your head. Break that ugly face of a cowardly Jew. And what can you do?" they laughed. "Nothing. Not even your God will defend you, better that you pray to ours. Say, My Jesus. Say Maria, Virgin. Say Holy Spirit! You shit. I'll pull out that disgusting beard, one by one those monkey curls! Say Jesus and you're saved. We'll let you go."

Roth, pious, small, frightened, and faithful to his God unto death, clamped his mouth so tight, it deformed his face, upright in the midst of the muddy water, with his wet caftan, eyes closed, ready for execution, seemed to say that his hour was come according to God's will.

What courage; I envied him. I would immediately have said "Jesus Christ" in order to get out of that freezing water, to not be in such pain, so helpless and ridiculous. God would understand that he'd been forced; a betrayal is something else, not that.

"Leave him alone," said some kind soul who was passing by, the boys with a final splash of water and an ultimate menacing threat took themselves off, for that day, and old Roth murmured a prayer, raising his eyes to the cold, rainy sky.

Instead of thanking the peasant, I said to myself, he didn't even look at him, he owed everything to God; the next time, that peasant would leave him in the water. Since his goodwill wasn't even worth a word of thanks, he'd become indifferent, rotten like the others, he was already known as someone who defended the Jews.

"They'll pay! They'll all pay someday," you thundered and comforted me as if you were God Himself, and I believed you.

"You'll pay too," you often said to Papa, who was capable of arriving late for Yom Kippur, and instead of pronouncing the words clearly, because of his black soul, he swallowed them, ate them as if it were just any prayer, then imagined that God would pardon him!

"What is God's forgiveness?" he'd asked you. "Is it like confession and absolution for a Christian? We're forgiven only once a year, if we're forgiven. And they are forgiven all the time, every day."

"God is already too good," you answered. "If a man shrugs off his sin every day, then he'll commit it every day."

Often, to defend Papa, I'd tell you about the fathers of my friends, pious, bearded, always bent over their books while their wives worked at home or in the store, and their terrified children went around on tiptoe, not able to say a word to them, fathers who weren't there for anyone. Wasn't Papa better? At least he was there, if only for a little while; you could harass him, he didn't frighten anyone, not even the fly that buzzed around him.

I wouldn't have wanted to be the daughter of any of them. I told you that. And you answered . . . would God that I were the daughter of one of those God-fearing saints, real Jews, to take your hat off to. For you humanity was divided between people who were good because they were believers, people who were bad because they didn't believe, and anti-Semites whether they believed or not. Or believers in an untrue God, who had provoked our persecution.

"I would never want to be the daughter of someone like our Hebrew teacher," I would say, offering my worst example, and you would defend even him against me. How could we ever have got along, we two? Still, Mama, I want to make peace with you without selling you my soul. I can move toward you, but you come toward me too. Do you want me to fast at least till noon on Yom Kippur, the way I did as a child? Do you want me not to eat pork? All right. I agree. But let me smoke on Saturday. Do you want me to light the candles on Friday night and not eat bread on Passover? Without bread, I'm always hungry, wasn't it you who said that without bread there's nothing?

You won't see this through with me, will you? You want me to be the way you want me, in your image, I have to deny myself to please you or you'll deny me. Let's meet halfway. Don't judge me. Leave everything concerning me to God. Let's us two make peace. Let Him decide if I've been a good Jew or not. I'm only repeating what you told me all my life, leave me in God's hands, and bless me, absolve me as I am, without making me pray or repent—and for what? My sins are ridiculous, it would be a waste of time for God to have to judge them, choose, indicate left or right.

Irma, our lunatic, told me that God tears the eyes from the dead in order to see better, that same tremendous day that she announced the end of the world was arriving for the Jews. I would survive but you wouldn't. I didn't even ask about Papa, because I ran home afraid of not finding you, to find out what you and Papa were whispering about in bed at night, which must have had something to do with what Irma told me: a great danger for us. Afterward I forgot her prediction, as you forget what a fortune-teller says.

Is it possible that you didn't know anything? You deny it the way the Germans did after the war, who didn't know what was happening behind their house, under their window, before their eyes.

How could you have been so passive, deciding also for your children that there was nothing to be done except to wait for the end? Yours, ours. The world stood watching; you waited, praying, invoking a miracle. And the global madness was committed. The Germans only executed what the world allowed.

If I think about it, I understand why the Israelis call us sheep, leftovers from the ghettos and the Nazi Lagers.

But I ask myself how someone could expect that from one day to the next they would knock on our door and say: Everyone get out, pigs, dirty Jews, and they would address Papa with disrespectful familiarity, and you, Mama, cursing our God to your face.

And you, poor soul, didn't seem to understand, you revolved, gesturing like a blind person who can no longer orient herself in her own house. You set yourself to collect here and there the most useless things before being driven with kicks from your poor nest that without you seemed cold, dark, dead at one blow.

For four years you'd been waiting for the fatal dawn. Four years with notices of new unstoppable massacres, while you saw us grow for nothing, to die. As long as others are dying there is always hope, right? If our neighbor dies, that suffices to make us feel safe.

If you knew we were condemned, why weren't you gentler, more loving, permissive with us children, innocent victims? Even prison guards are kind to the condemned. Not you, Mama! Until the end you oppressed us with your preaching about faith, honesty, rectitude, purity of body and soul, you did nothing but prepare for the great day of judgment. What difference did it make if my schoolmate threw me in the mud? What did it matter if they spat on me, what did poor Roth's humiliation matter, or your daughter's split head? Never return a blow, a good Jew ought to bear the punishment and leave retribution to God, it amounts to turning the other cheek. And your back—life on earth was hell, heaven paradise. Mama, Mama, how much wasted faith! This is what gives me no peace: your immutable faith so betrayed.

You never had a single doubt ever, a moment of uncertainty or revolt, only some protests, a few humble complaints to the Omnipotent, may His name be eternally blessed, sometimes asking Him why we had deserved so much evil and misery. What evil had we done? Poor you, what evil could you have done?

Your sins, if they are sins, were only with us, your children bent to your will until the end, when you told me: "Go! Obey! Go on. Go away, obey your mama." And I did obey. And because of that I lived. And I'm happy to be alive. You gave birth to me with unspeakable pain for the second time.

Do you think I'm not grateful? Is everything I've written and felt for you not worth a single Kaddish?

You seem like the Roman head rabbi who cares only for rituals, whoever performs them is Jewish, feeling Jewish doesn't count. Whoever defends Israel in all her wars is a good Jew; whoever criticizes it betrays her mother, father, country, history, herself. She is an outcast of the Left.

Being Jewish is difficult even among Jews, Mama. If you don't believe me, go to Israel for a while, Mama.

Sometimes I ask myself if the Promised Land is worth the price. If losing the image of innocence didn't take away our true identity, if it didn't divide us into Israeli and Jew, though for most people it makes no difference.

"A Jew shouldn't think aloud, shouldn't write certain things," you want to say. The usual phrases. "And before speaking or writing something, he or she should think twice." Isn't that true? You're a master in putting me in the wrong. Any sort of Jew is enough to put me in the wrong.

"I've told you something . . . Have I asked you for anything but a prayer?" A prayer. Only one. That's how it is. Only one. For you. What would be the point?

"Try and see," you encourage me as if in a game. "Come on . . ." You motion to me as mothers do when they are encouraging their children to take a first step alone.

"Try." You smile as you did in the photograph. It's incredible how beautiful you are. And sweet! How can I resist you? And how can I resist the paradise you must have found if you insist so much!

You're silent? You don't say anything. You act mysterious as always. You keep the secret to yourself. Certain things you don't say to children or you don't want to lie to me anymore? Oh don't be upset. Where is that angelic smile that cancels every rage in me, that urges me to keep you, to find the prayer book? Where did I put it? Do you want me to say a Kaddish? A prayer never said by a daughter for a mother.

Do I owe it to you? Is it the debt I have to pay you for my peace and yours?

"Well then?" you say, shaking me.

Mama Mama, I defend myself and wonder where I've put the prayer book, in order to say a prayer. Just to say it for my mama. You are losing patience, you are not listening to me. Are you returning to the dark because I hesitate? Prayer is a serious thing, Mama. I'd like to tell you this—you, who wouldn't notice if the whole world collapsed while you were praying. I've already told you that. I know, I remember it well.

"Unhappy creature . . . ," you murmur to yourself, looking at me with the pity you would have for a paralytic one couldn't ask to walk, only Lazarus raised himself up, they say.

Don't pity me, Mama, I don't need it. I'm strong enough to live and die by myself, though it's easy to say it because I'm not alone and someone will offer his hand at the moment of passing. It's like the rich who say they wouldn't mind if they found themselves suddenly poor. It's easy to imagine what's improbable.

I'm grown, Mama, but at the same time I'm very young, as I was when I lost you, and I wish you would be good to me. That you would look at me kindly, that you would smile at me again with that smile I discovered in the photograph, with those velvet cheeks, the cheekbones illumined by that mystery vibrating beneath your skin like a child's with a secret life. I know I'm talking to myself. You're not listening anymore. You're far away even if you haven't moved waiting for the Kaddish. If you want, I'll recite you a Kaddish! Yes, I! Here. At my house.

Don't tell me it's forbidden. That we need the temple. And a minyan. Otherwise it isn't worth anything. It's another sin. A blasphemy. Don't tell me that the voice of your daughter that has invoked you for forty-four years is worth less than the voices of ten men, strangers who haven't loved you, known you, felt anything for you.

Say yes, Mama, believe in me a little, come close. We are both tired.

Sit down. You've been on your feet since I started to write you, and I am too, in a certain sense, on tiptoe in my mind.

You sit and I'll go get the book. I had one with a red, hard cover. Where could it be? I can't find it. I never see the book I'm looking for.

Don't gesticulate at my shoulders, don't be impatient, I'll find it, if it was there, it must still exist. No one prays in this house. No friend has asked to borrow a prayer book, so I must have it. Don't say anything, Mama. Don't comment. For once be quiet. Have faith. What you don't find in a lifetime of searching reveals itself in an instant. You groan, watching at my heels like a secret agent, you want to catch me in the act.

Where would I have put that book the last time the books, black with dust, were dusted? What a disaster. Here. It's here. I told you. I want to sit down, too. Make room for me. My head is spinning. I have the sensation of being on a seesaw thrown off balance, alone. I'm about to fall. Sit, Mama, on the other side. For once obey me. Let's play a little. One time. For the first time. Pretend that I'm your mother and you're my daughter. Don't be afraid, no. The Kaddish prayer is yours, there, give me a push. To and fro, to and fro, harder, higher, harder harder, nearer to God, Mama! Nearer. I want Him too to hear my prayer:

Yis-ga-dal v'yis-ka-dash sh'may ra-bo, b'ol-mo dee-v'ro hir-u-say, v'yam-leeeh mal-hu-say, b'ha-yay-hon uv-yo-may-hon, uv-ha-yay d'hol bays yis-ro-ayl, ba-a-go-lo u-viz'man ko-reev, v'im-ru Omayn . . .

Magnified and sanctified be the Name of God throughout the world which He hath created according to His will. May His reign come speedily during your life and that of all the people of Israel, Amen . . .

TRACES

Happiness is born from loss,
What is lost is eternal.
                    —*Walter Benjamin*

I'm stretched out on the sofa. Through windowpanes, which are indelibly streaked, I watch a solitary pigeon outside on the red roof. In the faded blue sky, swallows chase each other. Swallows? I'm not sure, they might be called something else. I don't know the names of the birds. I love them. I am fascinated by them. I would like to know what they say to each other as they fly. How they manage to survive at the mercy of man and nature. I think I love all animals—the slithering ones less because I can't see their eyes. And I dislike people who hide their eyes behind dark glasses, mournful mirrors blackened by God knows what guilt.

The epigraph, which Bruck ascribes to Benjamin, is actually his quotation, in a letter to Carla Seligson in 1913, from Ibsen's play *Brand*.

I've seen far too many eyes in my life, and yet I can't remember my mother's eyes! My sister insists that they were violet, specked with an intense blue. My brother says they were blue. The only way I can imagine them is black, tinged by her thoughts, rarely smiling. Who knows what they were really? I don't know anything anymore. I ask myself how it is possible to forget the most loved and feared eyes of my existence. I ask myself uselessly. My memory is vague, lazy, burdened by too many things piled up, by too many uncertainties. In this absolute silence, I exist as if in a bunker, jumping at any noise. A sudden amnesia would truly be a vacation for me.

The pleasant emptiness I feel is disturbed only by a general uneasiness that I can't pin down. Reality and my own thoughts escape me. There is a kind of short circuit in my head, as if disturbed by static. One memory displaces another, the thread of memory tangles. I can't follow any thought backward. My route is obliterated. I don't know what's bothering me in a state that otherwise I could define as ideal. I am almost happy, with an irrational happiness whose source I am unable to name.

From outside there is only the noise of water flowing endlessly from an ancient fountain beneath the street. I don't just hear it, I know it's there, that it's mine. Perhaps I'd hear it even if all the fountains of Rome went dry.

My life, my past, seems suddenly dark, flattened, crushed under black unbreakable glass. A relic. A thick fog that gave birth to me, its daughter. This strange reality sometimes seems liberating, sometimes frightening, as if I were on a precipice. I try not to pay too much attention to my sensations, which are probably fleeting, like everything else. I force myself to be calm. Let myself live. I'm only too aware that this day will pass, as all the others have. Maybe I need to rest. I close my eyes. Without wanting to, I think of my age. I'm fifty years old!

So many years, and so few, I don't know . . . I am living them. Instead of simply stating my age, I confess it, admit it almost as if it were a crime. Something stolen. I am immediately invaded by a deep shame, like a traitor caught in the act. I have a need to justify myself, to explain to someone, but to whom?

I stop by the door of my bedroom, and my eyes fall on the familiar images of my dead. They provoke no thoughts in me. No emotion. They are like the noise of the fountain, something that is part of me. They circulate in my blood.

Maybe they aren't other people, they are my interior tenants. Me, myself. I return to my favorite place on the sofa, which is pushed against the wall. From here I survey the entry into the sitting room, where no one enters except the cats, who are now sleeping on my bed. Even when I go out to eat, I choose a place I can watch from. If I can't be on the lookout, I eat uneasily and leave quickly.

Suddenly a female voice breaks the silence. Shouts a name similar to mine: Katia or Tatia. I go to the window. I recognize the lady I've seen before, walking four straggling dogs tied by one leash.

One always succeeds in getting away. It's the black one with the short, shining fur. I would never have imagined that it was a female.

It's always she who escapes, maybe so she can hear her name called. She takes a leap, turns around, wags her tail, anxiously waits for the lady to call her, moves her ears happily, almost smiling, barks, shakes herself, turns back, and escapes again.

As I am going to lie down, I step on one of the cats, who, awakening, have drawn near me in silence. They meow because I bump into them, as if it were my fault.

The strangest thing happening to me is the general apathy I feel along with a sensation of well-being. At bottom, I'm fine where I am. In my own house. My longing for different places, for loved faces, now lost, is something nebulous that no longer torments me or makes me suffer. Something must have happened to me without my being aware of it.

From the courtyard, from one of the illegally built apartments under the roof, I think I hear the sound of a cello. I wonder where the musician lives. Maybe I hear him play even when he isn't there; he's been practicing for years.

A siren rends the silence outside for the millionth time. It's the police. Or an ambulance. Or the antitheft siren of a car, or a house, or one of the bolted shops. There are always alarms from somewhere. Day and night. They even set themselves off in anticipation; they're suspicious, provident, and unpredictable. Even things are afraid. Sometimes I feel as if I too am a thing, an object with conditioned reflexes, automatic, memorized. I execute what I must, mechanically. My flesh-and-blood image feels disfigured—changed into something unreal, uncertain as if altogether unidentifiable. The body! Maybe the body could become a map, a compass, a fertile terrain that could replace a memory tired of having to remember.

Without realizing, I start to sing. I sing a psalm I learned from my mother.

> O Lord, oppose those who contend with me,
> combat those who combat with me.
> Hold up your shield,
> rise to help me.
> Brandish your spear, bar the way to those who follow me.
> Say to my soul: I am your salvation.
> Let those who attempt my life
> Be confused and shamed.
> Let the Angel of the Lord scatter them . . .

I am happy. I weep with happiness. My eyes are wet with tears that don't want to flow. They stick to my eyeballs. They thicken. Tremble. They form a kind of female figure who floats on the pupils like an astronaut in space. It must be my mother. It is round, white. The form wavers, comes apart, pops like a flattened bubble, and the hot tears fall into the sink. The figure forms several times, dissolving more rapidly. It slides down my neck to my mouth, I swallow it quickly, as if parched by thirst.

I look at my bare feet. They are swollen. Tired. Enlarged. I've gone from wearing size 37 shoes to size 39! Even 40! Especially in the summer when it's too hot. I do nothing but buy shoes, sandals made of leather, fabric, silk, and they all hurt.

They pinch my feet, they wound me, they cut into my skin, give me blisters. There are no shoes in the whole world that will feel right. I have a closet full of new shoes that I've never worn except to try them on. At first, after a few steps, they seemed fine, then they turned out to be uncomfortable, unbearable.

I no longer know what size shoe I wear, I no longer have that security: somewhere between 38 and 40, according to the season and the pain I feel.

My hands, like my feet, are larger. From year to year, I have to enlarge the rings I wear; the gold is thin by now, so thin the rings are almost buried in my flesh when I wake up in the morning, if I forget to remove them the night before.

It still happens sometimes in winter that my hands regain their original appearance—slimmed down, beautiful—but my feet have become unrecognizable.

I'm sleepy. A cloudy substance is descending over my eyes. It thickens. It's a material that darkens; I could touch it with my hands if I had the strength to lift them. Better if I offer myself, if I let myself be wrapped around by this infinite veil that is stretching itself out over my entire body. I surrender. I let myself go, sliding into the shadows. I am already dreaming. I am conscious of dreaming. I'm waiting but I don't know for whom, or why.

I remember that the man in my life lives nearby and should have come down. I decide to go up to the top floor. I find myself in front of a closed door. I look for him, look around, give a glance at the terrace and see with surprise that it has a roof and is enclosed by thick walls of glass.

There is no sign of him. I call him, but I have no voice. I look for him but don't see him anywhere. I scream. I scream louder, but it isn't I who screams. All around me the place is deserted. I'm afraid. He really isn't here. And I don't know where to find him. I become aware that the silent screams are mine.

I wake up in turmoil. I can't breathe. I don't know where I am, whether it's night or day. I throw open all the windows and immediately shut them. I walk here and there a little to flee the dream inside me. It follows me, precedes me, persecutes me.

They are all traitors, I think, the living and the dead. Or am I the one who betrays them by not being able to cry for them anymore? Is it the dead who have eaten my memory? Just as hunger and flame have eaten their bodies. Now they are really dead. I can no longer remember their faces. I no longer pronounce their names, like the name of God. Mourning is over, or does it demand silence? Maybe I ought to pray. Beg the dead to appear. But I don't know how to pray.

How many times have I tried to do it? I don't know the prayers by heart. I never learned even one, except for the one you say before dying. My mother had the foresight to teach me that one at least. Faced with a prayer book, I stiffen. My body feels invaded, constricted by punishing wires that take away my sight and make me mute. As soon as I think of faith, I rebel against God. As if he were a family member who has betrayed not only my faith but my mother's.

Maybe memory is faith. Maybe it's necessary to find faith again by reviving memory. Who knows? Even this nothing that I feel inside me could be faith. Could it be that by letting go, by losing everything, one can find everything again?

I could write a letter to my mother. I've never written her. Why don't I write her? What's stopping me? Reason? Maybe reason is wrong.

I'd tell her everything that I want. Everything I'm thinking. I never said anything to her. I only asked her for something to eat and to wear and I begged a little love.

Somehow, she took care of the food, she darned the clothes, but love, she said, is for the rich, who have nothing else on their minds.

Dear Mother, dearest Mother, most loved Mother, adored Mother, Mother unknown, Mother always in a rage, Mother of so many children, Mother ashes, Mother! It's no good. How can I call you? To write to a dead person is crazy. I'm not crazy. Maybe the crazy are just without memories, maybe the craziness of the world resides in not remembering.

Dear Mother, I have to write you. Dear Mother, what should I say? I'm the age you were when you died. You were so young . . . and you were old to me. I want to tell you that I'm all right, even if today I feel lost, without memories. In my room, I always have your photograph in front of me, enlarged to giant size, and it no longer says anything to me. You stare at me with those retouched, alien eyes and that thin mouth that isn't yours. Maybe this is why you are silent, because it isn't you. More than you. I recognize the holiday dress you're wearing. The image of my father at your side is also silent. He is so serious. He looks into the void with an ivory face. Dearest Father, can I call you by name?

Mama, I never told you about my house at the seashore, it's for sale but it's still mine. So different from your house on a muddy plain. In May, the most beautiful month, there are broom plants, yellow as the star you sewed on my vest. It's the same yellow.

The border shrubs are pittosporum, another plant you don't know, one that makes me drunk with perfume when I awaken.

There is so much land that you could even cultivate tobacco for Papa, there's myrtle, thyme, rosemary—with violet blue flowers like your eyes, Mama, if my memory doesn't betray me, but it does betray me. For you who used to divide your little garden into small plots of carrot, celery, parsley and had your hen's corn for a border, all this unused land would be a waste, a sin, an affront to God.

But there are also figs, Mama, which you've never tasted. And almonds, which you've never eaten either, and there are the walnuts, prized for your desserts, but above all flowers, Mama, trees, useless things to you because not edible. And nectarines, a bastard fruit but marvelous, with a tasty yellow pulp. How I'd love to have you taste one. Goddamn it, how I'd love that. Forgive my bitter blasphemy. The fruit from my trees moves me more than your photo. But how is that possible? What's happening to me? What I feel at this moment can't be true even if it seems as definitive, as immutable as your death. Amen.

I start walking again to move my tingling feet. My blood tries to circulate, to reach the seat of memory.

Where did I put my cigarette? Was I smoking? Sometimes I light two at a time, or I convince myself I'm smoking one when it's no longer lit. It's the effect of the nicotine; I don't know which is more lethal, the nicotine or the forgetfulness that is its consequence. At any rate, I should stop smoking. I will stop. But I don't know when. Already the decision to stop smoking makes me smoke more. I light another cigarette. I snuff it out and clean the ashtray. An acute pain makes me put my hand on my right side over my kidney. One of the many doctors whom I've visited in my life predicted that in ten years I'd be dead of a kidney disease. This happened at least twenty years ago. Meanwhile the doctor died. I've forgotten his name, he was a Pole with cold hands and an insufferable voice. Presumptuous, besides being a bad prophet.

"Your mother died from a kidney disease?"

"No, Doctor," I said, "she was gassed at Auschwitz."

He looked at me, disappointed at being unable to rebuke me.

I light another cigarette, and the tingling in my hands increases. I put it out immediately, because I feel sand in my eyes, like so many pins under my eyelids.

I press my palms to my eyes and think again of my mother in her ornate holiday dress with a white jabot under her chin.

I've always seen her—or, better, remembered her—wearing that good dress, the dress for grand occasions, funerals and marriages, or the day of Yom Kippur in the synagogue.

Maybe memory is conscience. The mind cancels or represses what it deems unnecessary or useless to remember. Even while denying it to myself, I do nothing but look for the reasons for this stasis, paralysis, arrest, which doesn't allow me to move either backward or forward. I should leave. But where to?

Aside from recent memories, the substance of my existence presents itself to me as a block made of slabs of a porous stone set one on top of the other and crumbling here and there. Maybe good and bad in equal measure result in zero. The accounts won't add up.

Strangely, for someone like me who has lived in doubt, everything that I think and feel in this moment seems definitive, absolute. Without possibility of evolution. And this is unbearable.

My present state could also be defined as that of a traveler longing for a station where trains neither depart nor arrive.

I could call it limbo, a neutral terrain without a precise landscape distinguishable on any side. What time can it be? Two. Only two.

I begin to search for something that will make me remember my mother better than the photograph; I ought

to have in a drawer a shawl or cap, something that belonged to her. Rummaging, I find a purse that isn't mine,
forgotten by who knows whom and left for who knows
how long. Suddenly I remember Giorgia, a young friend I
haven't seen for years. It must be hers, it's all made of jeans
fabric, blue and shining as she was, egotistical and generous, present and absent, seductress and betrayer—just like
her that evening, who knows how many years ago . . .

"Let's drink," she said, and I agreed, taking the bottle
from her hand as cold as my right side. She looked at me
with her clear, exaggeratedly blue eyes and ground her
teeth like someone with a high fever. She had delicate
rosy skin, slightly freckled; the veins stood out clearly on
her fragile neck. Under her blouse, her immature nipples
hardened at the slightest touch. She sucked the cognac
from the bottle as though it were a nursing bottle. A sort
of friend-daughter, a rebel angel who wanted to leap the
prohibited ditch with me, hand in hand. While we drank,
we laughed and our complicity was stronger than shame.
We kissed each other, undefended. She ravished me, then
afterward we lay next to each other, silent and guilty.

Since then, the purse had lain forgotten at the bottom
of the bureau. Intact. Closed. Mute. I would like to touch
it but I hesitate, arrested in an anxious immobility, and
once again I get the sensation that comes when I'm in
front of my books or the prayer book. That I also felt

when I held Giorgia's hand while in secret she aborted
the baby she'd conceived with a stranger. I looked at her
sleeping face with the delicate features that reminded me
of Desdemona, an innocent victim. Her hair, ordinarily
smooth and bright, was ruffled, knotted by the terror of
that small, hard gynecological bed. Her long legs spread
before an image of a crucified Jesus, while a doctor, all in
white and all the more anonymous behind a mask, acted
magician-like in the most absolute silence. With the ra-
pidity of a Lady Macbeth, the assistant cleaned the bloody
things. The doctor disappeared as he had come, without
a word, face, or name. Giorgia's body, like a saint's body
in a procession, was raised and carried into another room
to wait for a taxi that would remove us through a back
entrance as quickly and as far away as possible . . .

Georgia's purse is filled with something unknown.
There is an object that I feel from the outside, weighing
it with my hand, and it has the shape of a weapon. I open
the purse; it's a gun! What did Georgia need a pistol for,
to kill or be killed? What difference does it make?—an
ugly, black, menacing weapon in my house. What horror! What madness! Where to take it, where to hide it?
I must get rid of it, I'd rather touch a poisonous serpent.
Maybe it's loaded and will go off, or I'll shoot myself. A
shot into this head without memories and that's the end.
Or I'll leave, I'll leave right away.

The cats run up to sniff the unknown object in my hand, diffidently they get closer, they look at it with dislike. Move away, puff, swell their tails, arch their backs, withdraw recoiling, hair erect. "Come on, come on," I encourage them, "there's nothing to be afraid of," and I reach out to caress them with my free hand but they draw back scornfully. They are in a state of war with the gun. Having reached the wall, they face me crouched as if for an assault. I hold the weapon in my right hand pointed at the floor. I could stick it into the oven since I don't use the oven. No it would be better if I went out right away and presented it to the police, telling them that it is an old weapon abandoned by a friend long ago, telling them the truth. No, they wouldn't believe me, instead they would suspect me of who knows what. They suspected me even when I was robbed, they asked me for documents, which, given that they were in the purse, I couldn't present! I even had to find someone to testify who I was. That I was I. I could have been a crazy person, a drug addict, a terrorist, a pathological liar—but not a robbed innocent.

Rather than go to the police and tell the truth I'll throw the gun into the Tiber. Not now while it's light out, tonight. The hand with which I'm holding the gun begins to swell, I have to move it. I pass the gun cautiously to my other hand. No, I can't throw it away like this, my fingerprints are on it. What do you remove prints with, alcohol, gasoline? I could clean it, make a package, and send it to the police at the central bureau. Via San Vitale 5. I'll never forget this address. Maybe because in places like that, one never feels adequately prepared, a stamp is missing, a signature, a document, a date, a stamp that validates the document, a receipt. Bureaucracy nurtures itself with bureaucracy. Everything needs a corresponding nourishment, war needs soldiers, power needs power, the slaughterer needs victims, money needs money, love needs love.

Oh God, what now? The telephone is ringing. Who can it be? "Hello hello!" On the other end of the line no one answers. I worry. Could the telephone be broken? I call 161. A recorded message gives the exact time: four o'clock, four o'clock. It keeps repeating the same thing. How long a minute is! It is always four. I hang up. What will I do with the gun? Here is yet another trial. Now I have nothing in my mind but the gun. I'll keep it. I'll decide when I get back. I always hurry my decisions. Rather I decide first, before others decide, because I foresee their decisions. I act instinctively, like an animal. The hour has come to take a trip in memory, a voyage thought about a thousand times and put off a thousand times, for forty years.

The gun will stay home, it's better. Who knows if I wouldn't shoot it there, in the place where they did their best to kill me? I dress. I go out immediately. If I don't buy the ticket now, I'll never buy it. In a great hurry, I arrive at the railway station. I arrange the trip for tomorrow morning at 8:05. As soon as I put the ticket into my purse, I calm down, like someone who has done something heroic, met a challenge.

At home, I check the date and the hour of my departure innumerable times, as if not trusting my eyes. I finally did it. I let the people closest to me know of my decision, to verify my unexpected plan, which makes me strong and vulnerable at the same time. Michael, my husband, isn't surprised; from the time we met he has known that I dreamed of making this trip without ever having the strength to do it. He understands that now it has become necessary, and although he fears for me, he encourages me to go. He'll take care of the cats, they won't be alone. Enviably, they are always sleeping.

Benedetto, the man who lately comes and goes in my life with the steps of a dancer, apparently always cheerful, always content, always smiling, he too is understanding. Fortunately neither of the two men asks why I'm going. I wouldn't know how to answer except to say that I have to go. To return in order to go forward.

The next day, I open my eyes at just the moment when the radio alarm is filling the house with bad news. The cats run to greet me, to wish me good morning just as they have done for thirteen years. I try to calm their meows, joyous and anxious because they know I'm leaving. They know it as soon as I pull down my suitcase. They don't let me get it ready. They sit inside it. Search in my purse, spill out the contents. With every glance, they complain about my departure, are easily offended, follow me everywhere and hide when I want to say good-bye.

Even though I have plenty of time, I'm overcome by haste. I want to be already at the station, on the train.

The telephone rings! I think immediately of Michael, who in a few minutes will come to pick me up and drive me to the station. But instead it's Benedetto, who wants to say good-bye, to know if I've slept well. He's afraid that I'll say no, that I haven't managed to sleep, but I tell him yes, I've slept a little.

"Sweetheart," he says, gently, hiding his admiration for my courage in setting out alone, "will you call me as soon as you arrive?"

"So late? Where?"

"At home. Even at home . . . What are you wearing? Make yourself beautiful, well made-up, put on your tan skirt with the maroon sweater. Or the maroon skirt and the blue-green sweater. Green-blue suits you. Though you don't seem to understand that. How do you have your hair? Comb it with the part on the side and the little braid I like."

"All right, fine, but now I'm cold, wet, I was in the bathtub."

"Make the line darker under your eyes and put a touch of dark on your eyelids, also underneath; it hides the circles, your tiredness. You are so beautiful when you make yourself up."

"I'm cold."

"Cover yourself. I'll call back, I'll call you back. What time are you leaving?"

"Soon."

"I'll call again, wear your blue-green sweater. Promise me?"

"I don't know . . . What if later I can't keep my promise?"

I hurry anxiously down the hall. I'm cold and sweating. I return to the bathroom and make myself up carefully. I look at myself in the mirror and find myself looking surprisingly well. Ready for the trip. I wouldn't change my mind for anything in the world. I check my new European passport, the train ticket, my reservation. I straighten up and empty all the ashtrays. I already have the first cigarette of the day in my hand, and outside it's still night. Once again I hear the sound of the telephone. The cats are frightened. They're right. They hate that ill-timed sound, it rings when it shouldn't and is silent when I'm waiting for a call.

"It's me." I hear Benedetto's voice again. "How are you? Are you ready? Calm, eh? All right? You are small but greathearted. I'm also small but greathearted, we're two small and exceptional people. In ten minutes you ought to leave the house."

"I know. I know it all too well," I answer laconically and a little annoyed, because Benedetto is always joking. It's fine to joke but I wish that sometimes he would let me talk truthfully and listen to the end, not avoid what is important as if it were fire.

"Are you dressed the way I told you? What time is Michael coming to get you?"

"Now, soon."

"When you get back, I'll come to get you. I'll let you know. I'm not sure yet. Maybe yes . . . let me think. Yes, yes, I think I'm free, but . . ."

"Ciao, ciao."

"When are you coming back?"

"What do you mean when am I coming back?"

"Yes, yes, I know, but what time?"

"At one, if everything goes all right . . ."

"And why shouldn't it go all right?" He laughs and jokes, and I seem to see his lovely smile, his white shining teeth.

"It will go just fine. Laugh! Sweetheart . . ."

"Ciao. Ciao ciao. Ciao. I'm hanging up. Hang up."

"You hang up. I'm hanging up . . . Ciao."

"Yes yes, ciao then." I barely keep my patience.

I check the time again, it's late. I'm not ready. And the buzzer is already ringing. Or it's the garbageman who rings all the tenants. It's Michael. "Just a minute. One minute." I yell into the intercom, "I'll comb my hair . . . what? The taxi is already here? I'll be right down." I run to hug the cats and can't find them. I bid farewell to the house, the objects, empty the last dirty ashtray . . . Michael takes all my bags. He won't let me carry anything, as though I were an invalid he was taking to the hospital. In the taxi we look out without speaking. The shops are still closed. I observe the few passersby, the traffic slow as on a holiday, a bleak holiday, perhaps because of the raw autumn weather that weighs on Rome like her history.

"If you're not all right, you can come back on the next plane," Michael says finally. "Or you can get off at Florence or Bologna if you change your mind. Here we are." He goes ahead of me toward the inside of the station. He gets onto the carriage with me. Arranges the baggage. Gets down. Gets on again with a bundle of newspapers and some candy. He is amazed that the compartment is still empty.

"If no one else comes, change carriages. It's a long trip. Don't stay alone. It's so hot. Everything smells bad, don't you think? Wasn't there a better train?"

"Barbara always travels on this one. She says it's the most direct."

"But what does Barbara know about it? Her friend, what's her name? She is a little more practical."

"Hertha. It's almost eight o'clock. Get off."

"It might be late. I'll wait."

"No, go, it's moving."

"Ciao, come back soon." We kiss. We look at each other. "One more kiss," I cry, as if I'll never come back, never again see that dear face, too much loved and never left behind.

The train gives a shake, hardly a start, like a warning. And stops. No one has entered the compartment. I sit on seat 46 next to the small window, its panes dull, milky. I feel the urge to touch it, sketch something the way I did when I was a child, a heart or a tree or a house. I don't know how to draw anything else. At school I had one bad grade, in drawing, the only spot on my excellent record. But I retained the desire to draw something on windows. I would sketch a heart, a tree, a house right now if I had the strength to move, if I didn't feel bound, constrained to rest immobile like a convict transported from one prison to another. I don't even dare light a cigarette, even though I know I'm in a smoking carriage. If only I could stretch my hand out to my bag, in which I have a little of everything: bread, cheese, hardboiled eggs, ham, fruit, sweets, and medicine. Medicine for pain of every kind. Since sitting down, my gaze has been fixed on the corridor from which no one comes. It seems as if I'm the only traveler on this train that should leave at any moment. I could still get off! No, I won't. I can't. I feel strong, even though fearful as a child dressed up as an adult.

We haven't left yet and already I miss Rome, my house. To think about my house, to know it's there, is to loosen the stranglehold that's taking away my breath. I would like to move, raise my hand, and trace a heart on the milky window with my index finger. A heart that's full, big-bellied. I can do it. Through the lines of the heart I look outside where it is all gray, cloudy. As a child I saw the snow on our neighbor's roof. A white peak on top of the heap of manure that kept falling into our courtyard despite my mother's protests and curses against those who felt free to invade our little garden. Mama never rebelled against heaven, expecting from it every justice, every hope of punishment, if not in life then in death. And there, beyond the heart I can see my husband's tense face etched for a moment, his lips move in "Are you sure? Are you certain?" and I signal, yes, that I'm sure, that it's a question of life or death. The train starts, accelerates, runs, leaves the station.

I've set off. I've already left Rome! I have a moment of panic and hesitation but the train knows nothing of it, it slides rapidly along its track as if it were lifted above the ground. I ask myself how I'll stay, how I can manage to stay. I wonder if they'll recognize me, if I'll recognize anyone. Suddenly the compartment door is thrown open and an imposing figure comes forward and questions me with his eyes. I reply that all the seats are free, there is no one here. "Okay, okay," he mutters and studies me from head to toe as if he were going to buy me. A woman's white head appears at his shoulder. The man comes in and unloads his baggage here and there, filling every empty space almost as if he were at home, lord of everything and I ought to be grateful to him for leaving me a little corner. He sits with his legs stretched onto the seat in front of him, barring the exit. His wife takes a seat next to his feet and opens a large book.

"Where are you going?" he asks me, almost shouting.

I look at him frightened, lost. "I'm going far," I manage to say.

The man scrutinizes me. "You're not Italian, are you? I on the other hand am. You wouldn't think so, would you? I was born around here," he says with emotion and in such a sad voice that he seems less huge and tall than before. "I ended up in Australia. I have an Australian wife. Stupid like all of them down there."

I look at his wife, hoping for a reaction, but she only sighs patiently, as mothers do with disabled children.

"Vacation, vacation, here's your vacation!" her husband assails her. "You've been wanting this vacation for ten years, to see your daughter with that German husband, German!"

The veins on the woman's forehead begin to throb rapidly like those of a lizard in my tomcat's mouth. My tabby doesn't hunt. I have to get up. Leave. Get into the

corridor this minute. I straddle the man's legs. Finally
I'm moving. What time is it? I look at my watch and find
it stopped at the hour of departure, and yet the train has
been moving for some time. The watch remained at the
time I have in my mind, the hour that has pulsed with my
heartbeat ever since I made the decision to leave, bought
the ticket. Something must have happened to the watch,
which has kept time punctually ever since my brother
gave it to me. A technological miracle like my clock radio, and now it has stopped and I don't know why.

In the compartment to my right, a man is intent on pick-
ing pieces of meat from a can with the point of his knife.
A little piece and a bite from a slice of black bread. Like a
soldier in wartime who consumes his rations a little apart,
hidden from hungry eyes. His figure and his gestures are
so familiar to me that I can't stop looking, convinced that I
have seen him somewhere. Maybe in a place where people
really died of hunger, of everything, for no reason. Who
knows if he would recognize me? Forty years are a lot—
though not for me. I can't see his face, he never raises his
head, from the back of his neck he looks like an old man,
but why doesn't he turn? I am struck by his Bavarian jacket,
too worn at the collar, his red-checked shirt that pokes out
at the bottom, his large trousers of an old cut but well pre-
served, his two-tone shoes. He is something of an adolescent in the way he carries himself. I wait, trusting that he'll

turn, recognize me, greet me. And what if I do it? If I greet him first, wouldn't he be forced to look at me and greet me too? He's got to turn around. Instead of opening my mouth I tap my foot hard to attract his attention. In fact I see him turning, a rosy color on his aging skin. His eyes, mild like a tamed animal's, almost sparkle, they are so blue. I stare at him. He too is staring at me and doesn't understand the reason for my look. Worried, he blinks, doesn't know what to do, he looks as if he were in a trap. He is embarrassed. Gives a slight greeting. I return it with a respectful bow. With reverence. Why? Neither he nor I dare move, to come closer. We remain silent like two people who look at each other but don't recognize each other, or prefer not to.

"Come in, come in, *bella Signora*." His voice, like an aged boy's, surprises me. He throws open the glass-paned door and bows slightly, like a clown, with a seductive smile. Hurries to dust the seat. I don't know what to do. I should go in. I make no resistance, I take a step. Enter. I sit where he wants me to, I obey.

"I've been to Agrigento, to our German cemetery, to find my comrades. Comrades," he repeated and he asked me if I'd understood, he wanted a confirmation. "You understand, yes?"

It's been forty years since I uttered a word of German, and now more than ever I'm unable to say a word, stupefied, incredulous.

I gather my strength, rise, and flee. Reaching the deserted corridor, I lean against the cold pane of one of the less misty windows and look out. If only I could get off! Wander in that countryside . . .

Suddenly I smell food. A smell like the one in my grandmother's little room. It smelled like that even afterward, when my grandmother had been dead for years. I would have liked to go to her funeral, but it wasn't possible, it was prohibited by law, my mother said, but the law didn't prevent me from following the funerals of non-Jews and so I followed those that I happened on, staying a little apart, like a stray dog. Cemeteries, death, that failure to return was an incredible thing for me. Extraordinary as a circus act, a sleight of hand. There had to be some trick, one couldn't just die and that was it. One wasn't there anymore. Didn't walk anymore. Didn't eat anymore. One would never return. It sounded impossible to me as a child and still does to me today.

As soon as I go back to my compartment, I smell the same odor, the scent of my fears, full of my apprehension of forty years, of my fear that grew lighter in the still air. As I move, I have the sensation of overturning something. My presence disturbs me, I want to undo myself, to disappear, but my attention holds me together, my nerves all stretch toward one end, to arrive. To reach my goal, as if I were in danger. Just as whenever I was about to die, I would think avidly of the few things that came to mind: my mother, my house, the village, and sometimes more hastily, as if taking time from death: the woods, the river, the school, the good teacher, the mean teacher. I felt sorrow for my life—not to be able to see the sun anymore, not to be able to eat bread, to grow, to marry and have children, maybe to die in my bed as an old woman like my grandmother.

Beyond the window a low gray sky unfolds, compact as lead. My mother knew how to read even the sky, she would interpret God's mood according to the color and the clouds. If it rained too much, it was His just punishment, the same if there was a drought. If it thundered, God was angry; if lightning struck, He was enraged with people. If a rainbow appeared, there was hope of pardon.

"At my house," she announced when I told her that God did nothing but punish and that not everything could be God's will, "at my house there is no room for doubt."

The Australian woman got up. She shivered as if cold. She began to rummage in one of the numerous nylon sacks that her husband had spread everywhere. She fished out a bottle of wine and thrust it at her husband. She didn't take anything for herself, returned to her seat, took up her reading, and it seemed to me that since we left she was still on the same page.

"Why don't you put on that damned thing my relatives made for you?" the man bullied her. She rose and, as if to silence her husband, drew a sort of shawl or small cape, it wasn't clear, out of one of the sacks. She put it on and immediately seemed ill, older; she resembled an old friend of mine whom I went to visit every day at San Giacomo's hospital. My friend always got sick in August.

"Is she your grandmother?" the other patients asked me.

"I wish!" I would say. "She's a friend of mine," I added, and this always led to some comment in the ward because I was too young to have such an elderly friend. She shrunk day by day, as if she wanted to scrimp even on her coffin, she who saved on everything and who gave to others what little she had. From beneath her sheets I would hold her feet, yellow and knotted, and massage them, and she laughed happily as if we were playing. She was serene, ready to live or die as if it were the same thing. She smiled at me as if she could smile at me forever. But as soon as she closed her eyes, it seemed that she would never open them again.

"Aren't you drinking, love?" I didn't believe my ears, the Australian man called his wife love. The woman is silent. She is punishing him. Silence must be her weapon; attack, his. The train enters the tunnel without making any noise, and speeds as if never wanting to stop again. I close my eyes and think of Benedetto, so sweet and gracious with everyone, for fear of losing someone. I think of Michael so solitary, isolated, defensive, so full of attentions to me, almost more than I am for him. Is it possible? "We'll get married," I said to him as soon as we met. "I'm not even divorced!" he laughed, incredulous, judging me a strange, willful girl, serious and infantile at the same time.

The train comes out of the tunnel. It immediately slows down. Stops in the open countryside. I reach the corridor and find myself face-to-face with the old German, the remains of an extinguished cigar slipped between his thin lips and false teeth.

"Why did you run away?" he asks, a little resentful. "I'm a gentleman, you needn't be afraid, I wouldn't touch you with a finger," he explains, touching me.

I draw back brusquely. I can't stand his touching me. He is surprised. I am surprised that he dares to be surprised. He ought to know who I am, that he harmed me, that I am the victim and he the executioner. Don't you remember anything any longer? Am I the only one who must remember?

"Why? Why?" he asks me in Italian, made almost desperate by my refusal; I give him a half smile as consolation, turn my back, and move away. I enter one of the empty carriages. I need to be alone. Not to see anyone. Again I want to be invisible to everyone. To vanish. Just as I do when I don't feel accepted, loved, or when I'm humiliated. I really want to say something to that German who comes from Agrigento where he has prayed at the graves of his comrades. If only I were able to say something, to formulate even one sentence in his language and pronounce it, it would be a liberation. A word would be enough. A language can't be guilty, even less can it be canceled and prohibited. Once there, I'll be forced to speak it. I see a boy pass in a white jacket ringing a bell for lunch. Who is he calling if there is no one on the train? It all seems completely absurd. Me included, on this train that goes to Germany.

"After Florence there will be the first seating," he repeats several times, and I'm happy to learn we are still in Italy. I'm aware of being extremely hungry. I go back to my compartment and begin to eat. And am unable to stop.

Here are the first houses. The station.

Voices with Tuscan accents. In the corridor I pass a young blond traveler holding a child by the hand. A man who must be her husband and resembles Gramsci follows her with his mussed head low; a black button of mourning projects from his jacket. The woman addresses her son in German, the man says something in Italian.

The last time I was in Florence, it was with Benedetto, who showed me the city as if I were seeing it for the first time, as if he had created that beauty by himself, including the *Primavera* of Botticelli in its restored colors. A sweet melancholy fills me for those days irremediably past and never relivable with the same intensity.

"What does that man have to offer you?" one of my single friends asked me, finding herself more alone since Benedetto came into my life.

"Joy. I want room to play. Lightness in living," I answered as if I were saying, Bread water salt air.

"Who is this man?" my brother asked, looking at me severely when he heard about Benedetto.

"What does it matter?" I answered, lowering my eyes.

"Yes, yes . . . I don't mind, but be careful," he warned without looking at me; with his eyes like those of my father when he gave me a stern look.

The train starts up again. This time the pleasing rhythmic shakes make me think of the rocking of a huge cradle; they take me back to my infancy. To note it down, I draw a pad and pen from my purse.

The Australian sticks out his neck, curious.

"What are you doing? Writing?" He wants to know.

"No, no, nothing." I defend myself and make everything disappear.

"Are you keeping a diary? Are you a journalist?"

"No . . . it's something . . . for me."

He looks at me and stammers: "For her, for her. One should write for everyone! Do you see the book my wife is reading? Everyone reads it."

With a glance I agree with him and close my eyes in order not to have a discussion.

The memory that I wanted to catch on paper flees, disappears. It will return; this is what the trip is for, for what else? I take off my boots, which are burning my feet. I huddle up as I do on the sofa at home. I think of all the accumulated letters that are waiting for answers. While waiting to leave, I did nothing. I think of all those notes I saw in Jerusalem stuck in between the stones of the Wailing Wall. I didn't know that the Jews asked for grace in writing and I found it so naive, so childishly innocent that it gave rise to a great respect. Even though I was tempted, I didn't dare take one note out to read it, to find out what you could ask of God. What did people ask for: love health money happiness pardon? A son? What would I ask for? One must ask for everything in order to have a little!

"Tickets please." A female ticket collector, in a uniform as dark as the guards' in winter, recalls me to reality. She asks everyone briskly, "Reservations too."

In a rush I can't find anything. I'm afraid of women, I've always been afraid of them. In the Lager, too. The bad women were always worse than the men.

"Where are we?" I ask her, to diminish my fear.

"In Bologna."

"Bologna?" I marvel. "But when do we arrive in Munich?"

"We're on time," she answers curtly.

"What time is it now?" I ask, to keep her from going.

She looks at the watch on my wrist and after a glance of maternal disapproval goes away.

"It doesn't work," I shout after her and find myself alone. Seeing that the baggage of the couple is all there, I console myself. They couldn't have got off.

I move to go to the bathroom, walking quickly to avoid any encounter. Yet on the way back, my haste provokes one. I drop my bag, and the German quickly retrieves it. I thank him. At that moment I don't recognize him, without the jacket he is thinner, less martial, two large suspenders hold up his trousers, they make him look like a scarecrow. He invites me to sit down with firm courtesy, then pulling a wallet out of his pocket he exhibits a card of a pale celestial blue. He tells me to open it. I read: Fritz Karl Beiger, born at Landsberg. October 17, 1910. He is over seventy years old. In 1944, I calculate, he was thirty-four, fully a man.

"Landsberg," I pronounce clearly and without upset, as if I'd been born there instead of having lived there as a prisoner.

"Landsberg!" He straightens like a soldier at attention, and his eyes shine at my familiarity with the city of his birth.

"This card is valid for a month," he tells me. "I could travel all over Italy but I've only been to Agrigento," and adds, "word of honor," as though I doubted what he was saying. "I was at Tobruk like Rommel." He has already assumed the tone of the veteran, he is evoking his past.

"Rommel," I say, amazed at hearing that name, and the old man is pleased that it's not unknown to me.

"*Jawohl!*" he insists as if testifying to something. "Praise God that it's over! Now it's the Americans and the Russians who are fighting wars, not we Germans. We had our dead too, but our dead don't matter. Every year for the last forty years, I've gone to Agrigento, and I'll keep going as long as I live. Understand?" He raises his voice and his index finger. "It shouldn't be forgotten. It mustn't be." He admonishes me. "I go to see if the cemetery is kept up, if the government money is well spent, do you understand? But what can you know of the war?"

I make a sign that yes, I know everything about the war, but he looks at me with disbelief. His face is pulled to one side and his cheeks redden, he leans toward me as if to discover where I've hidden my years. His breath smells of wine.

"Ah, you, *bella Signora*, back then you must have been still in your mother's belly. No! Still with Papa!" He laughs, and his allusion makes him blush.

I shake my head to make him understand that I was there.

"Do you have children?" he asks me. "*Bam-bi-ni,*" he adds in Italian, and without waiting for my answer he complains that the good God denied him sons.

I smile at him, happy to know that he has no children.

He is confused, not understanding the smile on my lips. He looks at me attentively.

"I bet you have a German mother whom you're going to visit, or a papa. Did you marry an Italian? You shouldn't mix races. Italian husbands are no good."

"No, no," I protest, and try to think of the best way to get out of there. He's a wretched old man, and my mother used to say that the poor have no time for reflection.

Here he goes with photos in his hand, the emotional moment is coming. He shows me one. He is in a uniform but not a soldier's, a large sack hangs from his right shoulder, he has some parcels. "Mail," he announces happily. First postman, afterward soldier, then once again postman. "Five years a soldier," he says with pride.

Only now I notice that hanging next to his head is a large leather bag with the neck of a bottle sticking out of it. The bag, though blackened by use, must be the same as the one in the photograph; evidently with retirement he got to keep the bag. Resistant, durable, eternal, incorruptible, like everything the Germans produce.

The old man is fingering a cigar. He cuts it in half with a small knife and puts the remaining piece carefully into a box painted with historical scenes.

"They're expensive," he says defensively, referring to the cigar. "Does it bother you?" At my distracted no, he lights up, keeping the burned-out match in his hand.

I think of the postmen in my village: they were like messengers of good and evil. I waited for them anxiously. And when I saw them appear over a hedge, I ran to meet them, dreaming of who knows what surprises and gifts. I even dreamed of them at night. At school I wrote themes about the postmen who were poor and had broken shoes and froze in the winter cold. But now the old man is showing me a second photograph, of an old woman with the look of a peasant.

"It's my wife, she's sick. At home I do everything, it's my duty, isn't it? Every year she has come with me to Agrigento. This is the first year I'm traveling alone. She can hardly walk anymore because of her arthritis. I even take care of our garden."

I feel trapped. I can't leave. He says that a husband ought to stay by his wife for life, because he has sworn loyalty and support. One's given word must be kept.

I no longer even hear what he is saying, I only want to flee, to slide from under his arms, which are open at the level of my head. I feel imprisoned by a sort of shame. I would hurt him if I went away again as if he had the plague.

Fortunately the train is slowing.

"Verona," the old man informs me. I take the opportunity to go into the corridor. "It's raining. It's raining," he repeats.

I get close to the window, but the frost that covers it keeps me from seeing out.

The old man is at my shoulder. He looks at me. Only now does he seem to notice my silence; surely he thinks that I don't understand German and that his tale was nothing but a monologue.

He looks at me with his small, light eyes, and muses on some strategy for staying with me so he won't have to be alone. He begins to enumerate every Italian word he knows: *"amore, bella signora, prego, buona sera, grazie, spaghetti, eccellenza, signorina, pesce, pane, capito, sì no . . . corna!"*[2] And he makes the gesture that signifies being a cuckold and laughs contently, amused.

He winks at me, as if to say that he knows other dirty words but won't say them out of respect. He starts to take my hand, to reassure me.

I withdraw again before he can touch me, and I slip into my compartment, leaving him confused and disappointed.

The Australian couple is asleep, she with her book in her lap, he stretched flat out, occupying my place as well.

I sit down next to the woman and, since I understood everything the old man said to me, try to exercise my German, at least mentally. I haven't forgotten the language but I can't speak it. It doesn't want to come out of my mouth. What if I were to try and sing? I remember a song that the

---

[2]"Love, beautiful lady, please, good evening, thank you, spaghetti, your highness, Miss, fish, bread, I understand, yes no . . . cuckold!"

soldiers sang while marching. It had to do with their home-
land, with happiness, with flowers. I sing it in my mind.

> In my house
> The roses open,
> In my country
> Happiness flowers.

I am not even able to sing. The German language affects
me the same way prayer does, I am filled with a bitter re-
belliousness, rage. I have never thought of any people this
way, of any country as I do of Germany. Germany and the
Germans are part of me. A German is necessarily a part of
every Jew's life. Does the German think so much about the
Jew? I've never imagined Germans other than those I've
known, and I see those Germans in every German, even
in Hertha and Barbara, who are my German friends. Am I
traveling to erase the memory of those Germans? To see a
different Germany from that one? Does it exist? Going to
Munich, or anywhere else, is the same for me, I could go
to Berlin or Frankfurt. For me one city is enough to represent all of Germany, and all of Germany is a German and
the Germans. I know it is absurd but it is like the innocent
language that I'm unable to speak and can barely listen to.
Just setting a foot on German soil will be enough for me
to feel I'm in all of Germany. It will be enough to cross the
border with one foot to feel I'm in a minefield. The first
astronaut on the moon must have felt less trepidation than

I do. I feel sick at the very idea of arriving. Still, I must go! In order to stop thinking about it, in order to stop being afraid of the lion, I put myself in the lion's mouth.

Maybe if I had made this trip with Benedetto, it would have been like a game. Munich would have become what it may be, a most beautiful city, and the Germans would be just like the French or the English, and the German language would be just one of the many languages that are spoken in the world. Instead of remembering all the words that I have heard—"Garbage, dirty dog, die, worms. To hell with you and your damn race. Disgusting Jews. We'll kill you all. You will die down to the last one!"—I would think of a poem of Heine or Hölderlin.

Who knows if there is still that great plaza in Munich where people searched in the ruins for food, for a bit of furniture to rescue, for a lost relative? It seemed strange to me that the Germans too were hungry and dying, and when I saw the babies, I thought I was imagining them. I couldn't understand how they could have been born or what they would do in this world of assassins and the dead. Who knows if I'd recognize a corner I'd seen before, a street I'd already walked. Will I be able to give thanks for directions, to give a tip, to buy things, perhaps go to the theater, send postcards to friends? Will I be able to smile? To say excuse me if I bump into someone? Offer a greeting when I enter a place? Will I know how to act like a normal person? I don't know. It doesn't matter. I'm not going to visit Germans or Germany, I go to visit my own self, the place of my rebirth. Without telling a lie, I could tell the old man that I was born in Germany.

At the Bolzano station it is no longer raining. The air is pure and cold. The sky is dark and sprinkled with faraway stars. All of a sudden the corridor fills again, animated by a group of youthful skiers; they shove and push, calling to one another, as if they were separated by a great distance. They occupy the empty seats, filling every space with their sacks and skis.

I am still in Italy, I could still get off, take the first train back to Rome, put the trip off, perhaps to the spring or summer, more cheerful seasons. The boys and girls speak German. They laugh at everything. They apologize while squeezing me against the cold window as they pass by. They keep talking, all together, and shift themselves so as not to be separated.

Even before his voice, the odor of his cigar announces my German . . . in the Lager you also said "my" when by chance a soldier chose a prisoner to whom he held out a few potatoes or left some scraps in the mess tin to be washed. What a struggle, what fights to defend your personal German.

"*Signora*," he calls at my back. I turn and see him on his feet at the door of his compartment, which is free of young people.

"Come in," he says, and indicates with his small eyes the empty seats.

He comes slightly nearer. I remain outside in the corridor and look at him through the glass of the half-open door.

"We're at Bozen," he informs me.

"Bolzano," I correct him.

"Bozen, Bozen," he repeats obstinately. "Not Bolzano." He smiles.

"Like Landsberg," I say.

"*Ja, ja*, naturally!" he affirms. "Germany."

"Like Dachau, Kaufering, Magdeburg." I name for him three of the more than one thousand six hundred Nazi concentration camps.

"Stuttgart, Köln, Frankfurt . . . ," he laughs, trying to teach me the names of other German cities.

I play too, and I think of my gun and my heart beats furiously while I name for him a series of cities and regions with their principal camps and hundreds of branches. If my words could fire, they'd kill him: "AUSCHWITZ BOBREK BABICE BUCHENWALD DORA ADORF ALLENDORF BAALBERG DORTMUND ESSEN LEIPZIG ILSENBURG SONNENBURG WEIMAR FELDAFING INNSBRUCK LOHOF OBERDORF SALZBERG FLOSSENBERG BAY-REUTH WINSENBERG NURENBERG PILSEN TEPLITZ GROSS-ROSEN CHRISTIANSTADT GASSEN GRÜN-BERG HIRSCHBERG FALKENBERG TANNHAUSEN

BERGEN-BELSEN MÜNCHEN! More?" I ask him with a look as furious and dark as when I touch a prayer book. Inside myself I add, "I have crossed the whole width and length of your Germany barefoot, do you understand?," and without being aware of it, I show him my feet in boots so new that it is difficult to think of them wretched, naked, full of ice, pus, blood, of snow, shit, and pain.

He backs away, baffled, perhaps frightened, overcome by all these names that I've drawn from the archives of memory, that I want to expel once and for all as if I were exorcising myself. The old man bends his legs and huddles in the corner, silenced.

He puts his hands in front of him as if I were about to hurt him, as if he no longer wants me to come near him, as if he doesn't want to see me, wants to distance me forever from his eyes, which have become cowardly slits.

Exhausted, I turn my back on him and take refuge in my compartment, uneasy. I feel bad, as if I have wronged someone who hasn't long to live. I curl up on the seat and wish I'd never said those names to him, and at the same time I go on mentally listing them: Majdanek, Mauthausen, Esterwegen, Hinzert, Ravensbrück, Sachsenhausen, Konigsberg, Lichtenburg, Salzberg, Linz, Theresienstadt, Furstenberg . . . The whole of Germany sown with factories of death.

Perhaps it was these names that have invaded and blocked my memory. My hand slipping into the pocket of my coat feels something hard, metallic. It has sharp angles and six points: it is the Star of David, my "cross," which unites suffering and hope. Usually I wear it around my neck, but this trip is special and I don't want people, seeing it, to identify me. It's gold. I had it made to order. Of my own free will. Just as I am going to Germany of my own free will. Even if it can't be seen, I feel that all of me is a yellow star.

"Passport please." The voice is courteous, but it gives me a start. I tremble inside. Maybe we've arrived at Brenner. I have a moment of bewilderment. Are my documents in order? I haven't done anything wrong, my passport is valid, I've paid for the stamp and I didn't need a visa, I'm free to enter and leave Germany when I want to. I'm an Italian citizen. A tourist like any other. I present the document to one of the policemen.

The husband of the Australian lady presents their passports with a confident gesture; the passports seem to me to be American. And are quickly returned.

They hold mine. The one holding it disappears. Why, what have I done, what's wrong? I look at the remaining policeman. He is wearing a cape over his uniform that softens it. They must be Austrians. There is something in their uniforms that reminds me of my grandfather. The other policeman reappears with my passport. I practically snatch it from his hand. The two of them go away clicking their heels in farewell.

I begin to prepare myself. I collect the magazines and newspapers, which I haven't even glanced at. It's the first time this has happened to me. Usually they keep me company, a piece of Italy in my travels. Reading the announcements, the names, the trickery, the sorrows and disgraces, I feel at home. I've carried bread with me, along with the papers. In Italy the bread is still good, the way the crust is slightly burned on top reminds me of the bread that came out of my mother's wood stove. Bread making was her great moment; master of the proper quantities of wood and flour, in control of the intensity of the heat, which had to be just right. She spent her brief existence saving, mending clothes, sighing, thinking of the next day. And daily thanking a God who left her in wretchedness, in thrall to cruelty and ignorance.

"What's the matter?" she would ask, annoyed by my continual requests or demands on the world or God, conscious of not being able to satisfy either my basic wants or my curiosity.

"Go to your father, he's the one who ought to earn, he's the one who has studied," she would explode, moving away brusquely. And I unfailingly returned to her because I was convinced that she owed me everything. Wasn't she the one who did the talking whenever she and my father spoke? Wasn't it she who gave us news of him when he left with the borrowed cart and someone else's load to sell? Wasn't she the intermediary between Papa and us, us and the world? Wasn't it she who had given birth to me? What did my father have to do with it?

"I came out of your belly," I answered her, touching it as if I owned it, my house before birth.

She was scandalized every time, as if I had blasphemed.

"I know, I know it," I laughed and clapped my hands, making her angry.

"It's God who has given me children, and God will take them from me when he wants to," she sighed, her breasts large and round as our bread.

"Is it God who sleeps with you or Papa?" I burst out, though I didn't know exactly what Papa's role was.

"Get out of my sight. Stop talking nonsense. Everything is God's work, on earth and in heaven," she affirmed, serious.

"Even idiots? Wicked people? The poor who don't have anything to eat?"

She gave me a withering look, then, sighing very softly, added in defense of God: "With everything He has to do, He can't think of everyone. If He wants things this way, He must have His reasons. He always knows what He does and why He's doing it."

I stared incredulous, and smiled at her slyly as if to say, "Don't make me laugh please, Mama."

"I have no wish to play," she said as she fled, reproaching me for always wanting to know, to play, to take her time instead of leaving her in peace to work. Unless I wanted to go outside with a bare bottom.

"In this house one can't ask a simple question, can't play or know anything," I protested.

"You will miss this house," she warned me, as if she were certain she would lose it.

"I can't even tell you that at school . . ." I stopped myself so as not to offend her.

She became alarmed. "What about school? What happened?"

"The teacher said that Hungary is a great heart with a piece missing."

"And then?"

"And then I responded that that was the reason it treated us badly." All the class laughed, and he got angry with me and hit me on the head with his stick and then shouted, "What is Hungary?"

"Great! Good!" they answered in chorus. But I didn't say it was good, only that it was big.

"Get up!" He grabbed me by my blouse and told me that a Jewess, just like all the other Jews, didn't care at all about Hungary's mutilation. And for punishment, I had to write a hundred times that Hungary mutilated was no longer Hungary, Hungary whole is paradise on earth.

"You always have to provoke them instead of doing what they want," Mama said, "instead of shutting your mouth and not even looking them in the face so they don't know you're there. What does it cost you to say what he wants?"

"What does it cost you to say that Jesus is the son of God?"

"You asked for this." She gave me a tremendous slap and became totally silent, suffering. I suffered too, waiting for her to open her mouth, to look at me, to pardon me for making her angry.

I look at the photo on the passport that I'm still holding in my hand. It seems to me that I'm looking at my mother. I resemble her increasingly. In certain photos where I'm too serious, I seem not even to be myself anymore, but her. When I smile, I seem instead to be the child in the one photo where we're together.

The train has passed Innsbruck and moves in the night toward the German frontier. Now I won't leave my compartment until I arrive. I don't want to see the old man again, and I don't want him to see me. I'm ashamed for him and for myself, I wouldn't be able to look at him, I don't intend to say good-bye when we arrive. Until I see him leave the train, I won't move.

"Good evening, *Guten abend*," I hear repeated in the corridor and see two soldiers appear who ask everyone if they have something to declare at customs.

No one says anything, I raise my shoulders, make a clear denial.

Except that in order to say it, I raise myself, stand up straight. I feel myself strong, ready for the battle that is uniquely mine. I'm not afraid or tired, instead I have a sensation of lightness, almost of well-being, I've crossed the threshold, and I don't feel anything except a great sense of calm. Hertha will be waiting for me at the station.

While I'm waiting to get off, I try to compose some phrases in German. Some simple phrases from a manual: Could you tell me the way? Please. No, no, I won't say please. Where is the English Garden? I'd like a latte. How much is it? Where is Maximilianstrasse? Thank you. No, no thanks. I will not speak a word of German. I'll use English: *Coca-Cola, sandwich, fast food, hamburger* are universally known words. Once mistaken for an American, you are instantly welcome. America was the dream, the salvation of Europe; but today the Americans too are afraid.

The Australian lady makes a farewell gesture, the unpleasant husband also nods to me. The old German passes in the corridor, but I don't move yet. I will be the last to get off.

From the steps of the train I see Hertha, who is worriedly looking for me.

She runs to meet me, pushing an empty baggage trolley in front of her.

She is more anxious to welcome me than I am to arrive, to set foot on German soil after the forty years of forced absence—a consequence of my first experience here.

She takes my bags from my hand. She helps me get down. If I were smaller, she would take me in her arms. As we walk she holds me up as though I were an invalid, or a child who is learning to walk.

She asks me in a maternal voice if I'm hungry, if I'm thirsty, sleepy, how the train ride was, if I encountered many Germans.

"Only an old man," I say laconically. "He was coming back from Agrigento where he goes every year on the day of the dead to honor his dead companions. Do you understand?" I ask her, for she doesn't understand Italian well or at least she doesn't seem to understand what I am trying to tell her.

"What is there in Agrigento?"

"A war cemetery."

"Forget it." She is annoyed. "Rest assured you'll be very comfortable here with us. I've made exactly thirty-nine phone calls to find a room in a good hotel."

"I'm sorry . . ."

"You have a beautiful room in the center, on Maximilianstrasse."

"Maximilianstrasse?" I marvel, having thought of precisely this street during my failed exercise.

The inside of the station is almost deserted. Outside, the city that I remember wounded and destroyed, its upper stories slashed off, inhabited by lost ghosts—this same city opens like a fan before my eyes in a pinwheel of multicolor lights, like a gigantic amusement park. It is all new, a theater scene, an immense Disneyland, a stage where something of which I was both protagonist and spectator is about to be presented.

I feel faint and clutch Hertha, my heart beating fast in my throat.

"It's beautiful, isn't it?" she asks.

"Yes, yes," I answer and see the old man coming toward me, he is almost here, perhaps he wants to greet me, perhaps to say that he is sorry, perhaps to ask for forgiveness. What does he want from me?

"Someone is greeting you, who is he?" Hertha asks.

"The one on the train," I say hurriedly.

"Greet him, oh," she makes a fastidious gesture. "The hell with it."

"No no, I can't, I'm not able to."

"Munich is beautiful, *ja*," the old man says with a smile and awaits my approval.

I nod yes, I almost smile back, I want to say good-bye, but when I see him make his farewell with a military gesture, standing at attention, I can't do it.

I watch him go away and am aware for the first time that he limps. It pains me, what would it have cost me to say good-bye?

Hertha guides me to her parked car.

She opens the trunk, extracts a magnificent bouquet of bridal flowers, and offers them to me, from her friend Barbara too. "And also from Germany," she adds with a forced smile.

"You aren't Germany," I say a little resentfully. She caresses my face as if I were an overly capricious child, sulky and hypersensitive.

We speed into the city that has something gay and festive about it. Perhaps this is because of the store windows full of food, clothes, jewels, flakes of artificial snow, Christmas trees that seem made of plastic, of little hearts and ornaments that announce the holiday to come. Everything is brightly lit—as if it were day; a stream of cars runs, ordered and silent on the wide, clean streets. After a bank, two banks, a church and another bank and three luxury hotels, Hertha brakes suddenly. She parks next to a coffeehouse.

Before getting out, I glance at my suitcase on the backseat.

"Here no one steals. We're not in Rome," she assures me, and I look at her again, offended.

The little room with its small tables and buffet is full of women who talk among themselves softly as if they were conspirators, friends, lovers, single women who meet each other there. Anticipating my gesture, Hertha rushes to light my cigarette. The little waitress with a lace apron offers us two complimentary aperitifs.

"Welcome," says Hertha, raising her glass. We toast, and she begins to question me as if she were a journalist, not a photographer. "What did that old man want from you?"

"He was a Nazi," I say clear and forthright though I feel ashamed.

"Oh, no, this had to happen to you, of all people. Did you tell him about yourself?"

"No . . . but . . ."

"Good girl! You did the right thing." She cheers up and pats me on the shoulders in praise. "Well, here you are and no one has eaten you, right?"

"Yes, I'm here but it doesn't seem real, I feel as if I were somewhere else, in a make-believe place, I don't know where, but not in Germany. Where is the bathroom?"

"I'll go with you." She starts to get up.

"No, no." I move away.

I sit on the toilet, which I find sealed with a paper band. The place is perfumed, furnished with all the necessities, even with a bottle of good cologne. I rest. I try to realize where I am. No sound comes from outside. Everyone is speaking in a low voice as if they were in church.

"Is everything all right?" I hear Hertha's voice from outside. "Are you all right?"

"Yes," I say and come out unwillingly.

Although I told her I wasn't hungry, that I had brought an abundant supply of food with me, she already ordered various dishes. She wants me to taste everything. I grant her wish so as not to disappoint her, it would seem almost like an insult if I didn't eat, if I said that the wine is bad and the food too sweet and that the bread smells of molasses and that everything has more or less the same taste. I don't even feel free to tell her that I want to go to my hotel, but she reads my every wish on my face. My spontaneous yawn decides her.

In the hotel they welcome me with big smiles as if they have been waiting for me for some time, as if they knew me already. I give my passport to a young lady who is all charm. Taking it, she wishes me a magnificent stay in Germany, "in Munich," she adds.

I thank her in English and look spellbound at the flowers, the colored carpets, the frescoes on the walls, the art deco vases, and the expensive velvet curtains.

The door of my room opens on surroundings created for an aristocratic young girl. On the round table in the midst of a bunch of little flowers, two packages stick out wrapped in silver paper tied with red ribbons. An envelope hangs from one of them. I take it, open it, and read, "Dear Katia! Welcome to Germany. We love you. Kisses.

Hertha and Barbara." I untie the ribbon and liberate a packet of salt and a chunk of black bread.

"Bread and salt," explains Hertha, "mean good luck in my part of Silesia. Our Silesia. They chased us out too . . . Do you know that we lost everything? My father was also killed in the war . . ."

I don't want to answer her. I don't want to tell her that the difference is that perhaps her father killed my father, who was unarmed, defenseless. I would like to explain to her that time can't wipe out the differences and confuse the stories. That Auschwitz isn't comparable to anything, but I prefer to watch her, as without waiting for my response she occupies herself with arranging the flowers, my clothes, my bed for the night, the bath with perfumed foam.

I keep thanking her, tell her that everything is perfect, that there is nothing I need, that she should go and rest, relax a little.

She leaves reluctantly, walking backward as if to take in the whole scene, to ask herself and me if everything is working, if I'm happy.

What was Hertha afraid of? What wrong did she possibly need to make up for? She was only four when I saw Germany for the first time. Her excessive attention only made me remember the opposite excesses, made me uneasy, created a sort of dependency in me just when I needed to feel free to face my ghosts, who would come back sooner or later.

Days ago, in Rome, I was in the office of an Austrian doctor who was examining the X-rays of a section of my spine.

"It's clear that you had an accident," he said, indicating the cervical vertebra.

"Me. Never."

"Try to remember. A car accident. A bad fall."

"No. Impossible."

"But I see it clearly," he insisted, almost accusing me. At that point the telephone rang, the doctor answered speaking German. Suddenly I remembered. "Yes, yes, I was hit in the neck with a rifle butt."

"A gun?" He put down the phone and looked at me in amazement. "And when?"

"Ah, a long time ago when I was barely more than a child . . . It was a German, right after I arrived at Auschwitz."

He remained silent for a moment, then asked, "How many times were you hit?"

"What do you mean how many times?"

"One, two, three times? Be more precise."

"Why? Do you think that at such a moment one counts the blows?" I stared at him incredulous, indignant.

I submerge myself head and all in the tub.

I like staying that way, it relaxes me, I am aware of the movement of my body, the beating of my heart, I feel pregnant with myself.

I raise myself up only when I run out of breath. I have scarcely lifted my head when I hear the sound of the phone ringing, oddly it seems to me, next to the flowers and the bread and salt.

Running, naked and wet, I reach the receiver and recognize Benedetto's voice. How did he know where I was? "Yes, yes, hello!" I shout as if he were far away and I hear his voice, calm, effusive, and unlike me speaking German almost with pleasure, talking to the hotel operator who doesn't know who I am or if I have arrived.

"She's probably in the bathroom," Benedetto insists; neither he nor the operator has heard my voice, I am excluded from the conversation. Finally his greeting and his questions about my well-being reach me, but I am not able to go into anything in depth, because he inundates me with his paternal cultural recommendations:

"Go see the old art gallery, the modern art gallery that was founded by Ludwig the First. And the Schack Gallery, remember Schack. Don't forget the English Garden, take a nice walk, Munich is very beautiful, you'll see . . . Climb the tower of Frauenkirche, from there you can see Isar, the snow-tipped Alps. Is there snow? Is it cold? Dress warmly and take a look at the City Hall . . ."

"I'm not here for tourism," I interrupt him.

"Yes, yes, I know, but don't miss the beauty. Sweetheart, go see the things I've mentioned."

"Yes, yes," I promise and am in a hurry to hang up because I'm soaking wet and getting the chair and floor wet and I must clean them right away, as if afraid of being scolded.

"The collection of Rembrandt!" he exhorts before sending me a hundred kisses, a thousand kisses, and I even more.

Finally I'm in bed, in an immaculately clean, perfumed bed with the down comforter similar to the beautiful one my mother had. Except now I can't stand down quilts, they suffocate me. I bought them in Hungary and in northern Italy, but I don't use them. Just as I don't use flannel sheets or the fabric that I buy on impulse, not for myself but for my dead mother. I have five lengths of fabric in my closet in Rome, and I don't have the heart to give them away, but sooner or later I'll give them to some woman in the countryside. My nightgown too resembles the single beautiful one made of lace that my mother possessed, that she inherited from her mother. It was like the wedding dress of a rich bride.

Instead of thinking about sleeping, I'm in a state of anticipation as if something might happen to me any moment.

On the bedside table I see a bible. I open it but cannot read it, even with glasses. The letters are fused in a single black line. Have I gone blind? I get up and run to look at myself in the mirror in the bathroom. I see myself. I must be tired. In Rome too, it happens—when I'm tired, I no longer see anything. I close my eyes. I'm happy to be where I am. It seems like a triumph. I have won. I'm in Germany. In a German hotel. In a German bed. I want to sleep. I will sleep.

I get up early and go down to have breakfast. While I eat quickly, I become aware that I keep staring, fixing everything that goes on in front of my eyes, searching spasmodically for something to discover. I have an ear open to every phrase pronounced in this tranquil place where they walk on tiptoe and speak with discretion.

I feel like a spy. A detective, a judge who wants at all cost to find the guilty one, who doesn't believe in the innocence of the accused and who knows that beneath the mask of appearance the truth is something else. Embarrassed, I prefer to leave rather than stare at an old couple in Bavarian dress and two serious men, perhaps businessmen, along with a gay couple and a group of Americans who are taking snapshots of each other in turn. I leave my key at the desk; fortunately no one is there.

Outside I am welcomed by a blue sky, high, limpid, full of sun in late November. I look around, it's still early, and the steps of the few passersby echo rhythmically. Their faces are closed and they walk slightly bent forward so that I can't search their faces though I want to—with the same inquisitorial impulse.

Serene citizens, well dressed, feeling secure about the ground they walk on. They seem in a hurry. They don't look at anyone, and this too keeps me from seeing them. I ought to have worn something showy, but they don't even notice the punks. They are used to everything. In order to attract attention it is necessary to stupefy, to strip naked or climb the Colosseum and threaten suicide. People don't look at each other anymore. This explains the phenomenon of cross-dressing. I realize with amazement that this is the first time I haven't been afraid of a new city, an unknown place, instead I feel able to walk where I want in a leisurely way, and able to find everything. Like someone who has seen a place in a dream and finds it again in reality.

I don't know how long I have been walking or where I'm headed, but I have the impression that I'm on the right street and in the vicinity of something I'm searching for.

"*You speak English?*" I ask a guard seated in a glass booth.

"*Nein English,*" he answers jokingly as he comes toward me. He has an artificial leg and walks with difficulty. Before he gets close, I leave; I hear him behind me babbling something against the American language or the Americans.

I turn to a young man in jeans and a colored jacket, but instead of answering me he shrugs, maybe he's an immigrant, his skin is too dark.

Not far from me I see a large square filled with trees. The leaves carpeting it are the vibrant rust color of certain trees that I saw in Ethiopia where, because of seeing too many people starving, I lost eight kilos. The spring-like air has brought out numerous old people, men and women with their dogs who dig frantically in the leaves as if they were hunting truffles. They throw the fresh earth into the air, sniffing and barking to let people know that there is something under there. Is it bones?

Maybe I too am walking on the dead. Maybe the dead are under the flowers, the trees, the new asphalt, the sidewalks. There must be millions and millions of dead somewhere. Maybe it is because of them that everything is fertile, and every plant is passionately loved by the Germans. I examine the faces of these middle-class retired men with newspapers in their hands and pipes in their mouths, and they are like all the other retired bourgeois taking the sun with their purebred dogs. Forty years can hide so much, mystify everything. How can I recognize my jailor? How can I say: "It's he! It's he!" At least the man on the train didn't pretend to be changed.

I see a group of robust men in orange overalls come toward me; they are armed with brooms and wheelbar-rows full of dead leaves.

They talk, speaking a Babel of languages: Arabic, Turkish, and Greek.

They are like a separate entity in this city that doesn't belong to them and doesn't resemble their dark skin, their burning eyes. I pass by and greet them. They greet me, leering. They are thinking of sex, the way men in Italy did thirty years ago when I landed there. Progress and wealth have lessened the sexual appetites of the Italians too.

Walking along a series of richly decorated windows, I stop in front of a store of photographic and electronic goods. The screens of the color televisions are on and show the same program, an evocation, on the basis of interviews, of one of those solid families who seem to have come out of a Thomas Mann novel. The old lady surrounded by portraits of her dead sons, officers of the Wehrmacht, and a couple of living nephews, one a doctor, the other an industrialist, who have reconstructed their grandfather's enterprise from the ashes. All done with a great panoramic display of ancestral rooms, sofas, paintings against a background of romantic music. The old lady is like someone in exile, she smokes using a long black cigarette holder and speaks of her dead husband with devotion. She has nothing to reprove him for except the overly harsh education of their sons. Other faces appear on the little screens, of women grieving for their husbands, fathers, brothers, like anyone grieving. Like me. Their grief is worth as much as mine, and this seems unbearable to me. It makes me ill. I'll never be able to compare their deaths. I turn my back on the television program and return to my inn, where Hertha will probably be waiting for me.

"Where have you been?" She scolds me and looks at her watch to make me understand that I'm late. "I've been here for twenty minutes. You've gotten to be like the Italians. Did you sleep well? Did you have breakfast? Did you see how many things there are to choose from? What did you eat? Shall we go?" She helps me into the car and promises to take me to a marvelous place. "And what do you think of this sun? I've never seen a sun like this in November. Three days ago it was snowing. Even the climate is celebrating your arrival, or have you brought the sun with you from Italy? Barbara sends you a kiss and expects us tonight."

"How is she?"

"Barbara? Well. She would have liked to come but she had to finish a painting. Let's go along the Isar. In a few minutes we'll be out of the city in the green countryside, you'll see the forests, cows and horses grazing, I know you love animals."

"Yes, more than people. But let's not go far. I don't want to go too far away.

"Too far away from where?" laughs Hertha, and touches my face lightly with a furtive caress before accelerating even more, racing on the straight and deserted road in the midst of fields. Here and there you can see, amid the green, multicolored houses full of flowers—like a giant coffin.

"Isn't it like something from a fairy tale?" she asks, pointing at the incredibly pretty and sweet houses.

"Hansel and Gretel, right? Look there." She indicates a little house entirely covered in green with neat windows veiled by immaculate curtains.

The courtyard is a model of order, the wood stacked in perfect rows, the work tools are hung in their appropriate places and seem conscious of solidity, utility, eternity.

"What are you thinking about?" worries Hertha, who is observing me the way I am observing everyone.

"Nothing, I'm looking . . ."

"Do you see that mural?" she asks, turning toward a small village.

"Dachau, Dachau!" I read out loud from a roadside sign and feel as if I am about to die. I feel faint, sick. My body feels nullified.

For once Hertha is distracted, enchanted by the murals. She limits herself to telling me that from there it's possible to return to Munich and from Munich to Dachau.

"Would you like such a house?" she enthuses.

"Yes," I say softly, "but not here . . ."

"Ah excuse me, forgive me, I wouldn't buy a house here in Bavaria either. I too am a foreigner here. You know I'm from Silesia. Would you like to go into the forest or over to the river?"

"No, in the forest no, the trees seem like an army in rows."

"Would you like a little music?"

"No. I only want to look."

"It's beautiful here, isn't it?"

"Yes," I admit, looking at an old baroque church, a castle on a mountaintop, a householder in Bavarian costume, and the peasants working in the courtyards.

The river, when we meet it, makes a circle; the bank is hilly and sprinkled with little houses hidden in the green.

"There are beautiful things even here, aren't there? Would you have believed it?" Hertha breaks the silence.

"And where is Dachau?" I ask.

"Nearby. Do you want me to take you? It's seventeen kilometers from Munich."

"Only that much?"

"Yes."

"It's so near," I marvel and I look around as if to recognize a road, a house, a stone.

I make out a housewife coming out of one of the fairy houses and behind her a man with a serious air wearing his green Bavarian jacket. They greet us politely. Hertha returns the greeting in a singsong voice, but I limit myself to watching them and asking myself which is the true face of a man, of a woman, of a child, or a people? It depends on circumstances, and it is circumstances that determine their behavior. Are those who create the circumstances the only guilty ones, or are those who submit to such circumstances guilty too?

"But what in the world's the matter with you?" asks Hertha, alarmed by my silent thoughts. She tries to distract me, to justify, to defend the Bavarians, the people she belongs to by this time.

"These people have reconstructed everything with their own hands, cultivated every patch of ground. They're a simple people, indefatigable, hardworking. You see how everything is clean and cared for."

"Yes . . . ," I murmur, and inside me something poisonous is growing.

"To hell with the past!" explodes Hertha. "Forget it. Don't think about it."

"There were so many of us," I say more to myself than to her. "They must have thought of some calamity, an invasion of monsters, a procession like one in the Middle Ages of lice-ridden people in rags. Barefoot, starving, crazy, ugly, bald, marching who knows where, we must have frightened them, beasts with human faces. If you could have seen how terrified they were at the thought that we would stay one night in their barns, that we might steal one turnip, that we would eat their meager leftovers. God, what faces they made!"

"They didn't do it, really, Katia, they didn't . . ."

"They studied us as if we had the plague, and with incredulous eyes they looked at us from head to toe marveling that we went on two legs the way they did. And disappointed, offended by this similarity, they retreated in disgust, they hid themselves in their houses, reclaimed their children, forbade them to get too near, closed their windows. Uselessly I hoped that just once, once they would talk to us, ask us who we were, where we came from, and our names," I lament breathlessly.

Hertha stops suddenly. We pile out. "They didn't want to know, wasn't that it?" she says, raising her voice. "Not knowing reassured them, didn't it?! Let's go. Take a walk along the lake."

On the bank there is only a man seated alone on a bench drawing seeds or crumbs of bread out of his pocket and throwing them to the birds who pass on the soaked gravel. He seems to be talking to them as well, but when we come near, he lowers his voice and eyes. He is dressed in holiday clothes of the region, with a new coat that is too big for him. He seems like someone from the south of Italy. He has a classical face like a Greek. He doesn't even look at us, absorbed, far from where he is now.

Hertha, who has gone ahead, signals to me to join her, she wants to show me something.

"Here. See." She shows me a heap of leaves. "Underneath are little flowers, everyone knows it and no one walks on them. Can you imagine anything similar in Italy?"

To tell Hertha that she is an unconscious racist would be a terrible insult. I prefer to be quiet and follow her in a silence that seems a wall irremediably separating us. When she decides to stop in front of an ancient castle whose lower story has been transformed into a typical Bavarian beer hall, I follow her without asking where we are or why we must stop here. Beneath a low arched ceiling a crowd is drinking beer and eating smoked meat. Everything smells of smoke and cabbage, including the people and their long overcoats hung up at the entrance.

"They're speaking Bavarian dialect, do you hear them?" Hertha informs me. "I can't understand them either."

"I have worked in a place like this." I had a flash of insight. "It was the house of the officers and their families, and we prisoners worked in a room adapted as a kitchen. We were so closely watched that we couldn't even eat the potato peels. Are we near Dachau?"

"Yes. But forget about Dachau. Don't think about Dachau now. It's my fault. It would be better to go home. Barbara will put you into a good mood. But first let's eat something. How's that?"

"No. Let's leave."

"Home? You don't want to see anything else here. All the villages are beautiful, Dachau is also a lovely old town.

"Let's go to Dachau."

"Should I take you?" Hertha's blue eyes stare.

"Yes, I think so, yes . . ."

"You're sure?"

"I can't do otherwise."

"Right now?"

"I don't know . . . yes."

"Let's go tomorrow. I understand that you want to go there. It's better that you go. You have to face . . . but I promised Barbara that I wouldn't take you."

"I'll go by myself. I'll find the road. I know it. I've walked from here thirty times when I had the incredible good fortune of working indoors, in this castle, close to food."

"It couldn't have been this castle, maybe you worked in the castle of Dachau."

"I don't know. It was an isolated place like this, with a courtyard filled with trees."

"It's late, if you really want to go today . . ."

Hertha takes the road back, driving much too fast. Her face is rigid, tense, mottled with red spots. She smokes continually, lighting one cigarette after another.

"I'm sorry. If you don't want to . . . let's go home. Don't drive so fast, do you want to kill us?" I admonish her, playing on the same sense of guilt that made her drive so fast.

"Are you afraid?" She gives me a challenging look, squeezing her thin lips tight.

"No," I answer her very calmly and I stretch out my hand to her tense neck, her hair, curly and furious.

With a change of mood she slows down, looks at me, and asks, "Would you make love with a German?"

"Oh no, I couldn't . . ."

"And with a German woman?" She blushes at the idea though she herself loves women.

"I don't know, I think so, but I've never thought about it. About men, on the other hand, I've wondered many times in my life."

"Do you like men a lot? You're very maternal and they're very infantile, don't you think?"

"Yes. But women, too, are often childish."

"Before going to Dachau let's say hello to Barbara, it's on the way, but don't say anything."

Hertha's apartment, where Barbara is staying, is in a complex on the outskirts of Munich. The entryway is a greenhouse full of tall plants, and from it Barbara's red head appears. Coming toward me, nearsighted and absent-minded as she is, she bumps a plant and overturns it. She bends to right it, excusing herself to the plant while Hertha runs to help her as if she were a wounded person. Barbara kisses and hugs me while Hertha rains reproaches. Barbara is dressed in a rose sweat suit, and her long hair is held by a clasp that is a heart covered with gold stars. She makes me sit and kneels at my feet on the parquet, just as she did in Rome, and she lays her head in my lap and purrs, contented and gratified that I'm all hers for that moment.

Unlike Hertha, she doesn't ask me anything about the trip, she doesn't want to know where we've been and where we're going. She doesn't want to know anything, only to laugh and joke and act like a capricious clowning child in order not to think about anything and enjoy life.

"Ah!" It occurs to her. "I have something for you." She speaks in Italian and is pleased to speak it well enough, even with typical Roman expressions and accent.

From a box, she extracts a series of small cats cut from old velvet resembling the fur of Siamese cats; they are very similar to my cats. I miss my cats now and wherever I am.

"They're for you. Do you like them?" she laughs, contently rubbing her abundant breasts against my knees and sinking her face, round as a Flemish Madonna's, into my belly.

Next to Barbara, buttery and opulent, Hertha seems even thinner, her face like a sculpted cameo.

"Leave her alone," says Hertha to her friend in a maternal, slightly severe tone, perhaps jealous.

Barbara tries to caress her, but she withdraws brusquely in embarrassment.

"Do you see what the Germans are like?" Barbara says to me. "Vicious, bourgeois, and hypocritical?"

"Oh stop it," shushes Hertha. "Don't start with your idiocies."

"It's the truth, dear."

"How's your mother?" I ask Barbara to avoid one of their extemporaneous discussions—not infrequent, according to Barbara, who carries her love for women like a banner while Hertha denies it even to herself.

"I feel sorry for my mother. She still keeps the photograph of Hitler on her bureau. Every time we see each other and something goes wrong, she can't forgive us for being born, but we three illegitimate children, abandoned when we were small, must forgive, forget, and not ask her for anything. We are her guilt, her shame," she concludes.

"Let's go," says Hertha, annoyed, but just at that moment her neighbors ring and burst in. They are a couple with a little girl with two thin braids just like mine when I was her age. The man literally falls into my arms, kisses me effusively, and I notice that his breath smells of wine.

"I'm Bela," he says to me in Hungarian, leaning heavily against me. "My name is Bela," he repeats, his voice broken by emotion.

"You are his country to him," says Barbara with a smile. "I told him you were coming. He must have seen you arrive."

"For my husband to see a Hungarian is like seeing a member of his family," says his wife in German.

Even the little girl throws herself on my neck, and as soon as I sit down, she begins to do my hair, taking apart and redoing my braid as if I were a doll.

Hertha, constrained by the role of hostess, comes and goes, offering them things.

We toast once, twice, three times, and hunger grips my stomach. I ask for a piece of bread and Hertha butters it for me. She says that the German butter is excellent and I ought to take some to Italy.

"We are foreigners, exiles," Bela says, looking at me drunkenly with eyes full of desperation.

"It has been terrible for my husband to live far from his country," interrupts the wife. "Has it been that way for you, too? We're all refugees, foreigners . . . I'm from Silesia, like Hertha. I too lost my home."

"Be quiet," her husband exhorts her.

"And I who am I? Whom do I have? Only my mother and my father. No uncles, no grandfathers. I've learned about things," she says to me softly, speaking only in German without knowing if I understand her or not. "When I saw a film after the war, I asked my mother, Mama, but what have these people done?"

"Leave her alone." Bela, rising up unsteadily, tries to silence her.

The woman tosses down another glass and continues: "My mother answered that those things were the business of the men alone, that women had nothing to do with them."

"When I left Hungary in '68, I was twenty-seven years old," Bela manages to say. "We're all far from home."

Hertha becomes aware that the guests have dripped wine on the table, on the carpet. She runs with a rag and signals to me that it is time to go.

"I have a great admiration for your people," whispered Bela.

"For us. Who?" I ask him.

"I was in Israel for eight months. My firm did installations there, war stuff . . . electronics, I'm an engineer. We sell to the Arabs as well and install for them, but shhh"—he puts his index finger against his lips—"don't tell anyone."

"One more thing." Now the wife traps me and holds me down with no way out. "Do you think I would have been good or bad in those places?"

No one dares to name "those places."

"I don't know," I say in Hungarian.

"Long live liberty." Bela raises his glass, empties it, and smashes it against the fireplace, Hungarian fashion. Hertha stares incredulously. She murmurs something between her teeth about Hungarians and says that we must go.

"Where are you going?" Barbara wants to know.

Hertha makes a sign as if to say nowhere but it's time to get rid of the neighbors.

We cross a peripheral zone of demolition and construction, all cement and dust. From the midst of it a hotel rises, enormous and surreal in this withdrawn, uncultivated

landscape, suspended between a community of little one-
story houses and skyscrapers appearing out of the blue. I'm
not surprised that Dachau is located near this place, and I
think I recognize in some of the old houses something I've
seen before, small houses and courtyards that lack the appearance of wealth. Back then and still now, they remind
me of the village where my paternal grandparents lived,
and for this reason too I was astonished by those simple
people who looked away when they saw us pass and at
best threw us bread and then hid their hands. Maybe they
were as afraid of the Nazis as we were of the Fascists.

Hertha accelerates, pushes her way forward through
the intense and disorganized traffic until we come out at
a crossroads. Above us is an arrow that indicates Dachau
City Center to which all the traffic flows, and Dachau
Memorial, the ex-camp turned into a museum, where no
one is going and for which signs are posted obsessively
at every step.

"Here's the wall of the enclosure." Hertha drives around
a wall that seems nothing like Dachau's wall. It's rather
low and has none of the menace or insurmountable aspect
of my memories.

"The officers lived in that house," she says, showing
me a large yellow building that resembles the police station of my village.

"I don't recognize it," I lament. "Though I've cleaned those windows so many times, those stairs, the pavement," I add, observing the half-abandoned building.

"The entrance," announces my guide, precise and indefatigable. We are in front of a gate of wrought iron like that of an old factory.

Seeing my perplexity, Hertha states that the only remaining authentic element is the guard tower, and she points it out to me in the middle of an immense space buffeted by a malodorous wind.

"Do you remember it?" she wants to know.

"I thought it was taller. This way, without guards, lights, or pointed guns, it seems innocuous, almost like the steeple of a ruined church without the cross."

"Come, let's go in, the museum is here."

I begin to tremble but follow her without hesitation. And I stop next to her in front of a large panel with a black background, thick with the names of the German concentration camps, and there are hundreds and hundreds of white names, larger or smaller depending on the importance of those unimaginable places.

Stupefied, perhaps more than anyone, I look for my camps. There were seven of them, and I will remember their names even when I won't be able to remember mine.

"I can't find Christianstadt." I am alarmed, preoccupied the way I was when I couldn't find the name of a
city or river cited by the teacher on a map.

"It's there." Hertha points with her finger. "It's there,
part of Gross Rosen."

"No."

"After Bunzlau and before Dyhernfurth, don't you
see, here?"

"Yes, yes, there it is!" I'm content and, putting on my
eyeglasses, measure the distance between Christianstadt
and Bergen-Belsen, which I traveled on foot. On the map
the distance is short, but in memory endless. Suffering
prolongs time, while happiness shortens it.

Slowly, slowly, I find all my camps, they're there, they
are real, they existed next to large cities, in the heart of
small towns a few meters from the villages. Seen this
way, Germany was truly one big concentration camp,
and yet no one saw us.

"Dachau was the first German concentration camp,
built in 1933 for enemies of National Socialism and unde-
sirable elements." I hear the voice of a tourist guide at my
shoulders. I turn and see a young teacher with a group of
students: children of eight or nine, handsome, well fed,
in orderly lines, with faces that don't show anything, neither participation nor curiosity nor indifference; they are
only silent and disciplined.

"You can see historic documentation of the rise of National Socialism and the consequences," pronounces the teacher, indicating a series of photographs and documents. Two striped pajamas, two pairs of clogs, a whip.

The children look at what he tells them to look at. There is only the blink of an eye in front of a dead prisoner outfitted as a parachutist who floats in a tub of icy water. The heaps of corpses must seem like rags to them, broken marionettes with arms and legs twisted like those of acrobats.

"Children," I say to Hertha almost as if I have to confirm that they are real, but I don't see her right away. I find her to one side, diminished, contracted perhaps by the cold that begins to penetrate to the bone, perhaps by embarrassment.

Among the corpses in the photo I'm always looking for something familiar, a neighbor, a childhood friend, a schoolmate, but they have lost their faces, they all look alike, even the women and men.

"At Dachau, 31,591 registered prisoners died, plus those not registered," the teacher informs them.

What can those numbers mean? They don't mean anything to me. They are numbers. A large figure. They were numbers, and they've become numbers. Hertha signals me with her hand that we have to hurry, the museum closes at five: she shows me five fingers. She guides me to a door where a red light flashes like the light in a movie house. A screen projects images of the countryside flanked by fields of cabbages. Four horse-drawn carts move at a walking pace. Peasants with masks on their faces collect the skeletal corpses, which are lying at the edge of the road, and load them as refuse or as future fertilizer. Suddenly a dog enters the picture and seizes a foot with his teeth. His master swears and drives him away with a stick. In the foreground the masks of the peasants blend with the blinders of the horses. The scene changes, and as in a horror film we watch the hanging of three adolescents. Only now I discern in the darkness the lines of the heads of children staring fixedly at the screen in silence.

Hertha touches my sweaty hand with her freezing one to warn me it is time to leave.

"Let's go," she whispers in German. I get up and follow her outside. The wind, ever more furious, slaps my face. Earth and sky are the same lead color and seem to touch, to dissolve into a single mass, thick and heavy. Even the climate here is different; the cold that descends from the sky and rises from the earth seems unreal. The eddying wind starts up precipitously, keeping us from going on, or else pushes us violently from behind. The silence is so total, it is no longer silence but a cry.

Hertha and I clutch each other and advance down a central path, the ground on either side barely marked, like lots for so many vast, numbered tombs.

"They're the thirty-four foundations of the barracks," says Hertha, her voice swallowed by the wind.

"They seem like tombstones," I murmur, but my words are lost.

"I'm ashamed, believe me, I'm so ashamed of Germany." Hertha trembles at my side as I strain to hear words torn by the wind, which now whistles malevolently.

"It's the same wind," I remember. "It was the same."

The signs to the crematorium are marked incessantly like those on the road to the memorial. The arrows never end, faithfully precise, they guide us to a small iron bridge over a trickle of stagnant water. On the other side of the bridge we find ourselves in a well-cared-for garden with a low building in the shape of an L; it seems like a stable or nursery school. At the entrance is a statue of a prisoner with hollow cheeks, a philosopher, a saint, a revolutionary whose blind, empty eyes look at the sky.

I still haven't grasped where the crematorium is, and I'm already inside the building, which I would never have imagined holds four horrifying ovens with narrow mouths against which lean four narrow leather stretchers.

"They are authentic," murmurs Hertha, and my legs give way, I slide along the wall and look at the four crowns of faded flowers in front of the ovens.

"Do you see? Someone has put flowers," Hertha says, turning and stamping her cold feet. "Are you ill? What is it?" She is frightened.

"Nothing . . . nothing. I'm taking a little rest . . ."

"They close soon, if you want to see the showers . . . but it's not the way it was."

"No, no, let me stay here in peace."

"In peace?!"

My God, why don't I cry? I feel nothing, only a great emptiness, helplessness, and stillness, as if I were dead myself.

"Let's go," Hertha begs and stretches out her hand to help me up.

"I'm fine . . . leave me here, you go on . . ."

"Are you crazy?! We have to go or they'll shut us in here! It's nearly five." She taps her watch and her teeth are chattering because of the cold and because of the panic that contorts her face. "March! Get up," she screams in German, making even her boots resound. "March. Get going!"

I raise my hands in a protective gesture, and without looking at her, I get up and run outside, across the bridge. I enter the central street and follow it, my heart in my throat while Hertha follows begging me to stop, to wait for her because she can't run, she has a bad leg.

"Katia! Katia! I beg you. You know I can't run, I've been sick . . . Katia!"

"Die then!" comes to my mind and I immediately regret it; I stop and wait for her, embrace her. We hug each other, exhausted, united, and unmoving, fused into a single statue.

In the car, in the dark, without looking at me, Hertha murmurs as if to herself. I don't understand her but I don't want to interrupt our silence. I'm afraid to break with words the fragile thing that needs strengthening.

"Tonight you'll sleep with us." I am finally able to understand.

"No, I'm leaving. I'm going home, I have to."

"That's absurd." She is astonished.

"I'm leaving right away."

"And the hotel reservation for three nights? They'll make you pay," worries Hertha.

"I'll pay," I say, as if it were the final ransom for my freedom.

On the train everyone speaks Italian. They shout from one window to another with southern accents. Some departing woman, waiting with lowered head on the sidewalk, cries for her husband or her son. I feel as if I'm already home, as if I were in my family. I understand the bitter tears of immigrants, their looks, gestures, clothes, souls.

"Give me twenty marks," entreats Hertha, "a little tip and you'll have the cabin all to yourself. They'll put all the

Italians together to sleep!" she says breathlessly and goes to look for the person in charge of the sleepers. She returns right away, saying that it's done and I'm happy to know that even the Germans have changed, they can be corrupted.

"Was twenty marks enough?" I ask her with a satisfied smile.

"Ah!" She becomes annoyed and adds that the Germans too think only of money. "But," she whispers, indicating the attendant who is approaching us, "pretend you don't know."

"Thank you," I say in German, looking at him without him seeing me. "Thank you," I repeat, surprised at having pronounced my first word in that language after forty years.

Hertha has a reproachful look but she's happy that I've said at least one word in German.

"So you know how to speak."

"Yes," I calmly pronounce the second word. "But let's not exaggerate." I embrace her, say good-bye, thank her, all in German.

I shut myself in the compartment, stretch out on the bed like a woman who has given birth to a child after being pregnant for forty years. I feel a giddy sense of well-being, almost erotic as if someone had ironed my coiled nerves. My happiness at returning home is something that resembles those rare moments of total harmony in my life when I've felt at one with the earth, the sky, the sea, the trees.

No bed has ever felt as comfortable, as clean, and as accommodating as the one I'm lying in. If I were stripped naked, it would be even better, but moving feels as if it would break this enchantment, this enfolding peace. Finding myself already dressed would mean I'd arrive home sooner. Like a satisfied child, as soon as the train moves I close my eyes and don't know when I fall asleep but awake like a clock when they announce the arrival at the Termini Station in Rome. Those words sound to me like absolute truth, like the voice of God.

Seeing the city deserted, I think that maybe it is a holiday. I feel as if I have been away for an eternity, not a day. If someone were to ask me where I've been, I wouldn't know what to say, nor could I respond if someone were to ask me how the trip went. I don't know, what I feel can't be explained in words. Any phrase would diminish the simple sensation of being alive and able to return home.

With the same sense of malaise as when I left, I can't wait to shut the door of my house behind me. And see my cats again. Michael and Benedetto don't know of my return, and I don't intend to let them know. I need to be alone at least until the next day. I still have to take in the fact that I've actually gone and that I'm already home.

The cats, hearing my footsteps and the key turning in the lock, welcome me, but while I am cuddled with them in the entrance way, my memory betrays me, pierces me, beats me down: suddenly I remember that Dachau was the place where my father died! How often I've envied those who have a grave for their family members, with a name cut in stone that testifies to their existence and origins. How could I have forgotten? I ask myself. It is unforgivable. I should at least have brought a flower, but on which one of the thirty-four numbered barracks would I have put it? I should have brought thirty-four flowers, but I should have brought 31,591 for all the dead who were listed. I would have had to bring millions and millions to cover all of Germany with flowers!

Who knows, if I had remembered, I might have whispered a prayer that I've never said and never paid to have recited.

As if I need to hold on to something relating to my father's name, I run to my desk and look for the book that I'm writing. I'm as impatient as if I were going to find him, not just his name, which I've given to my elderly protagonist. I throw myself on the text like a starving person on food. I read:

Alex didn't seem to hear the joyous noise coming from the basement of the small villa, which resembled so many others in the residential area. Since he'd become ill,

with a sickness that you could simply call aging—though
he was only seventy-six and carried his years well—he
experienced reality in the present as something artificial
and fleeting. The past was more real to him than the face
of his grandson Jerry, who had shown up to check on
him just as he'd promised his mama.

"Okay?" asked Jerry, already impatient to leave. "Okay,"
he shouted more loudly, convinced that old people are
deaf. "I have to go . . . ," he complained, demanding some
sign of life from his grandfather, who didn't even look
at him but was staring fixedly at the rose-colored ceiling in the upstairs room. His daughter Olga had recently
moved him there to have him closer.

Jerry was about to go when his grandfather turned to
him, calling him David.

"I'm Jerry! Jerry! " The child stopped walking, irritated
by being called someone else's name on his birthday.
"Why are you calling me David?" He turned back. "Who's
David?" He became uneasy, perhaps sensing a presence
behind the name that he'd heard his grandfather say once
before when they were sleeping together. Another time
when Jerry had bronchial pneumonia, his grandfather,
who never prayed, prayed continuously for fear Jerry
would die. Approaching his grandfather's bed and bend-
ing over maternally, like someone leaning over the crib of
a child who is hiding a secret, Jerry asked for the millionth

time, in a sweet persuasive voice, who David was. By now he was convinced that a David must have existed.

"David was someone, right?" he continued coaxing his grandfather, partly from curiosity, partly from the slight anxiety he felt every time he heard himself called by that name.

With a reflexive look and gesture Alex asked his grandson to be patient a little, that he would tell him something but was thinking about how and what to tell him. He couldn't find, didn't know the right words for what he wanted to say. He thought that maybe they didn't exist in any language, so the fault wasn't his—even though he'd never really learned the language of the country where he'd lived for forty years.

"Well?" prompted Jerry, tired of this annoying delay, while below the guests loudly called for the birthday boy.

"David . . . ," the old man said wearily and stopped immediately although he was ready to go on, to compose a new, better phrase without errors of grammar or accent. Otherwise, as usual, Jerry would begin laughing.

"David . . . ," he began again, wrinkling his high forehead with the effort, but Jerry was no longer there.

"Jerry," Alex sought him, looking around with an expression ever more bewildered, because everything he saw, a gilded table, a closet with a gilded door, a gold telephone in the shape of a mouse, was alien to him, as if he'd never seen them before, never entered that room reserved for guests who never came.

Suddenly he raised himself from the bed as if to flee, if only he had an idea of where to go. He got down with surprising agility and stayed there to think of what he wanted and why he'd got out of bed.

Accidentally seeing his own image reflected in the mirror with a gilded frame, he became frightened. As if to reassure himself that it was he, he kept looking at that face, the white mustache, two intense eyes, some white wisps of hair, a skin pale and worn, though unwrinkled, that let the bones show through.

As if his image was no longer of interest to him, with decisive steps he entered the stairwell in the direction of the apartment below, where he once lived with Tamara, his wife, who died the year before.

When he entered the room where the children were celebrating, he was welcomed with noisy laughter, as if a clown had appeared in long underwear with a flowered pajama top that was too big and too lively for his eyes full of ghosts.

"What are you doing here?" Jerry stood in front of him, blocking him on the last step.

Alex, deciding to keep on, pushed his grandson aside without paying any attention either to him or the other children. He didn't hear the rock music at full volume or the television, which was on but ignored by everyone.

"Answer!" Jerry demanded, making his voice heavy, whether in defiance or because he was offended with his grandfather for not having told him who David was, or in order to amuse his friends, who would laugh to hear the Hungarian grandfather speak in his funny unnatural American.

Alex straightened like an officer and with quick steps entered one of the rooms, followed by a trail of children.

It was the bedroom, where he had lived with his wife, the first and only woman he had known in America. She was the daughter of the dyer Minsky, a Russian immigrant, who in order to help him took him on as a presser as soon as he landed in this promised land. Tamara, who had had polio as a child, was an only daughter with a slight limp, rather stupid and spoiled. Everyone said that with his background, it would be a piece of good fortune for Alex to marry her.

Quite a heavy past for the girl who had to try to make him forget it, but Alex spoke of it as little as possible in order not to upset Tamara with his terrible memories.

When Papa Minsky became aware that his daughter was not indifferent to Alex, he arranged the marriage with the good-natured Hungarian, handsome, serious, a good worker, and what's more, Jewish.

Speaking Yiddish, which the future son-in-law hardly understood, he made him promise as if it were a contract between them that his son-in-law would not talk to his daughter about the past. Minsky had spoken of it to her once and for all. In exchange there was the dye house that would one day belong to his daughter, the wedding expenses, and a house. Alex had to make two promises, three rather: to keep his memories to himself, to make Tamara happy, and not to speak Hungarian. And as far as possible, he kept his word. He put up with his hard-hearted wife-boss like a martyr, thinking that he wouldn't have been any happier with someone else, that he couldn't expect more than what he had, couldn't even imagine happiness.

While the children circled distractedly in that poorly lit room, Alex began to search for something with a feverish intensity, something so hidden and for such a long time that he no longer remembered where it was.

"What do you think he's looking for?" one of the children asked Jerry, but none of them could have guessed, because the old man thrust his hand into the most unlikely places, even under the bed.

"Let's go," Jerry proposed, afraid that his friends were no longer amused.

In fact their faces looked as if they wanted to flee, flee from an invisible shadow drained of color and painful in its dark stillness.

"Here it is," Alex said in Hungarian. He grasped a small box of carved wood between his hands. He closed the door behind the children and after a brief hesitation was about to open the box when on second thought he didn't, as if he were afraid to lose the contents. He stayed there with his head bent, silent. Pressing the box against himself, he put it into a pocket of his pajamas and left.

"What are you hiding?" Jerry stopped him again.

His grandfather shook his head as if to say, "Nothing, nothing," while he pressed his hand against the swell of his pajama.

"Show it to me!" screamed Jerry playfully. While another child pointed a plastic rifle against the old man's belly. The old man reeled, frightened, and almost fell.

The children, unaware of their cruelty, took the box from his pocket; they struggled to open it, until it opened by itself. Four photographs ended up on the floor along with mayonnaise and nuts and the remains of hamburgers and chocolate cake. Two smiling children appeared in the first photograph, a boy and girl of seven to eight years, dressed in sailor suits; a young, just-married couple smiled from the second photograph. The man had a mustache like Alex; the woman was wearing a short veil that revealed a sensual, happy mouth.

"Who are they?" asked Jerry, repenting. He gathered the photographs and, murmuring, "Sorry," handed them to his grandfather, who was still standing, petrified.

Alex, unsteady on his legs, wished only to move, get out, flee from these little assassins.

"Tell us who the children in the photograph are," Jerry insisted.

His grandfather babbled something in Hungarian and the children amused themselves by urging him to speak in that language; they had already forgot the photograph.

"Will you play something for us?" asked Jerry, pulling him along by his pajama top to a small piano that was part of the apartment's decor.

"My Hungarian grandfather can even play the piano," he proclaimed while he pushed his grandfather toward the stool and opened the keyboard for him.

At the sight of the keys, Alex put his finger on the *do* that began a child's song that he had learned when he was Jerry's age on the piano at home.

"Ta ta ta ta," he picked out with one finger, singing:

"Little spotted calf without ears or tail, ta ta ta ta ta ta and so full of spots. Why are you taking me to Pest: Ta ta ta ta ta ta ta ta!"

The children quickly learned the simple melody and sang along with *ta ta ta* but were quickly bored, and Jerry tapped the shoulder of his grandfather, who was singing by himself, to alert him that it was time to stop. Jerry shut the piano, helped him rise, and walked him to the stairs, pushing him with a "Quick, go" because he heard his mother's car outside. Jerry ran up to her in the garage. His grandfather returned to his bed with the box in the pocket of his pajamas. He covered himself well, leaving only his head outside. He closed his eyes. He didn't know if he should rest or pretend to sleep.

Jerry assailed his mother with a stream of talk about his fabulous party.

"Are they still here?" asked Olga, alluding to the children. "And Grandpa?" She was concerned that her father might have done something foolish the way he did the last time when he lost himself and couldn't even find his room. He was disoriented from the beginning in the new, overly large house.

"He got up and came down and took something from his old room."

"What did he take?" asked his mother, curious, but Jerry only told her about the little Hungarian song, which they had been able to pick up immediately.

"Ta ta ta ta," he sang for his mother. "Do you know it too?" he asked.

"Uh huh," she answered. "I don't know anything else in Hungarian," she said defensively, hostile to that absurd language.

"In a while Papa will be coming home. When are they coming to pick up the children?" she asked her son, biting a flake of lipstick on her thin lip.

With her chin receding to a short neck sunk between overly large shoulders and a small head full of long blondish curls, she resembled one of those girls who imitate a trendy rock star. She sighed as if she'd been walking a long time.

"I am going to Grandpa," she said to her son, who circled around her, disappointed at her slight interest in his birthday.

"Why don't you speak Hungarian?" Jerry asked her.

"Because I'm American," answered Olga, entering her father's room. At first glance it looked as if the man were asleep, or even dead, with his motionless hands outside the covers tightly holding something that appeared to be a box.

"Papa," she called him softly, as if afraid of waking him, or afraid that she would never wake him again. She didn't dare take another step toward that figure stretched out on his back with his head straight, slightly rigid, his face suddenly more youthful, calmer than usual, and far away. This image seemed so lovely to her, so new, so strange, that she almost asked herself if this was really her father. Even as a child she'd asked herself this strange question, above all when her father embraced her with his large, strong arms, making her feel minuscule, a mere nothing that he held to himself trembling as if he were about to lose her. Sometimes he squeezed her so hard that she almost suffocated and wanted to flee.

"Let me go," she shouted, twisting herself free of that embrace, which conveyed both love and fear. But at the same time she would have liked to be big and heavy enough to fill those arms. She ate constantly, never stopped even when she became an adult. She had become showy, plump, slightly hysterical, and always hungry.

"Papa," she called him again, risking a small step to the bed. She became aware of the box and stared at it, asking herself what it could possibly contain. Secret documents? His will? Compromising letters? Money? Jewels?

"Father," she said for the third time, and, encouraged by her own voice, tried to slip the box away from him.

"No no," protested her father, opening his eyes and looking at his daughter as if he didn't recognize her.

"I've just come back. Ben is still at the store, Jerry is downstairs. You know that it's his birthday, don't you?" she said all in one breath with the tone of a fearful child and at the same time protective. "Jerry told me that you got up and took something from your room. What did you take? What's in that box?"

"My children, my wife and I on the day of our marriage, my parents, my brother," her father said in his own tongue.

Olga, without understanding a word of what had been said, backed up as if she had been hit.

"But what are you saying, how are you talking to me, Father? What's happened to you?" she shouted so loudly that her son and his friends came running.

"He's speaking Hungarian!" she shouted, bewildered, raising an accusatory forefinger. "I don't understand him. I don't know what he's saying."

Jerry had an idea. "Let's record him." He took his tape deck from a companion's hand and put it beneath his grandfather's mustache. "Come on, talk."

The old man looked at the tape recorder with disgust, tried weakly to push it away, and after a brief incomprehensible mumble began once again to speak of his dead, silenced for forty years.

"Mama . . . ," he said, and Olga understood perfectly that he was talking with her mother. She was vaguely aware that her father had lost all his relatives in the Nazi concentration camps in Europe during the Second World War. For her as for so many others, this was prehistory, but she didn't know that her father had already been married, that he had had two children who were also killed.

". . . I've told you not to cry," the old man continued, always in Hungarian. "For a red ribbon . . . your hair isn't undone. How can I find your ribbon in this car. Don't you see that it's impossible? Is it my fault if I can't find it?" The old man's voice got louder, and everyone listened with bated breath, as if hypnotized by something they didn't understand.

For the first time Olga would have given anything to understand what her father was saying. And all of a sudden she felt resentment toward her mother, who had never wanted Alex to teach her even a few words in that language, because, she said, she'd had enough of her husband's attaching himself to every Hungarian client who came into the store. He was as happy as if he'd found a relative, gladder to see a Hungarian stranger than he was to see a member of his own family.

"David," said the old man, and he would have continued to say other things if Jerry hadn't interrupted him:

"He said David, Mama! Did you hear, Mama? He's already said it two times. Why does he always call me David?"

"I don't know," groaned Olga, ever more at a loss to think that her father had erased the English language.

She thought of having the recorded phrases translated by someone from the neighborhood who owned a Hungarian restaurant—where they went sometimes to eat—and made her father's eyes shine at every dish that was brought to him.

"Have you had other children?" Jerry asked suddenly, horrified by his own hypothesis.

"I?! No sweetheart. I have only you, what are you thinking?"

"Psst." Jerry bestirred himself, glad to be the only child, and held out the tape recorder to his grandfather who had once more begun to speak. He spoke of the war, of his children, of terrible things, his face gentle, serene, and free.

"I want to go home," he managed to say in English, then stopped, exhausted, while they were clamoring around him.

"Then he hasn't forgotten about us, or America!" Jerry said, brightening.

"I ought to call a doctor," Olga said to herself.

"David . . . ," his grandfather was beginning, and Jerry, irritated, made a brusque movement. The tape recorder slipped from his hand and fell to the floor, or Jerry let it fall, he himself didn't know how it happened.

"Stupid," his mother scolded, gathering up the tape recorder as if it were a relic. She tried to make it work but it seemed broken, mute. She opened it with an anxious gesture to take the tape, and realizing that there was no tape, burst into tears. Her son did the same.

Notwithstanding the optimistic predictions of the doctor who filled the old man with medicines to stimulate memory, it seemed that Alex had erased the language in which he had more or less communicated for the last forty years. He only managed to pronounce a few words, to say that he was all right, that he wanted nothing except to go home. To Hungary. To his own house.

Olga hoped that her father would soon switch back to English instead of continuing to speak incomprehensibly to all of them, including Jerry.

The boy now was amused to listen to him in that funny language that spoke of who knows what. Maybe tales. Or sad things? Sometimes his grandfather cried. Maybe, Jerry thought, old people are a little mad, not of this world. But he loved him more than his Russian grandfather; he preferred him because his Russian grandfather gave wet kisses.

Olga felt the double burden of taking care of an old man who spoke another language like a stranger but who was her father. It was enough to drive you crazy! She was neither a strong woman nor very intelligent; she had become somewhat superficial and spendthrift to please her husband. Ben wasn't sympathetic to his father-in-law, who didn't want to renovate or modernize the store when on paper it already belonged to Ben's wife. And therefore also to Ben. Ben kept suggesting to Olga the solution he thought would be the best for everyone: put the old man in a rest home with other Hungarians with whom he could speak Hungarian to the end of his days.

"I promised Mama that I'd keep him, no matter what," Olga defended herself whenever her husband approached the topic—practically every night. And always in bed, where Olga gave in to him more easily.

Ben had given in on everything, and in order to live quietly, let others decide for him. First his parents, who forced him to study law, because in a family of merchants it's always a good thing to have a lawyer—a satisfaction to a semiliterate immigrant father. Then his wife, who out of infantile jealousy and feminine possessiveness wanted him always near her. Because of an innate laziness, Ben left every decision to her, but when it came to his father-in-law, he returned insistently to the subject.

"Don't tell me again that you promised your mother to keep him," Ben raised his voice one evening. After much research he had found a sort of hospice that gave shelter to three Hungarians.

"Don't use that tone when you talk about my father. My father isn't a package, he's my father!" responded Olga, then she turned her back and didn't open her mouth again that night, although Ben, half repentant, pleaded with her.

"He wants to leave here. I'll take him to Hungary. Even the doctor says that a shock would be good for him. If his memory comes back there, maybe it will return here too."

"Oh, the hell with that." Ben thought the idea of the doctor and Olga was one of the most absurd things imaginable. And expensive besides.

"To go to Hungary!" he exclaimed, amazed by the very existence of a country somewhere in Eastern Europe that it would be better to forget and be sorry for those who had to live there.

"The doctor said that it's the patient's most fervent desire," explained Olga. "For me it's like granting his last wish, do you see?" she added woefully but determined that this time too she would convince her husband. Taking her father to Hungary would fulfill the duty of an egotistical daughter. And perhaps she would discover what her father had been hiding for so long.

"Okay," her husband conceded one night when Olga instead of opening her legs kept them tightly closed. It was his final statement after he had tried every way he could to turn his wife from the crazy idea of going to Hungary with an old man who was no longer rational.

"And how do you get to Hungary?" he asked, as if you couldn't fly to Hungary just the way you could to other parts of the world.

"I'll ask that woman who lives in Queens, on 160th Street, the blonde who lost her parents in a car accident three years ago, do you remember her? She found out from their will that they were Jews and therefore she was a Jew, and she found herself with Jewish relatives in Hungary, and now she goes there every year. What parents she had, poor woman, she's still in shock, it's terrible," commented Olga.

Ben didn't even listen to her, he limited himself to asking how much the airplane tickets would cost, and if they'd be allowed to enter the country.

"But we're Americans!" Olga was indignant.

"And who will take care of Jerry, the house, the store?" Ben was as fearful as a child in the jungle, having never done anything in his life except supervise the work of others, a frustrated boss directing the four employees at the cleaners. He was nauseated by the dirty clothes and the steam from the iron. The only thing that pleased both him and his wife about the inherited business was the money.

"You'll take care of everything this one time. The Portuguese lady, who comes to clean, will help you."

Suddenly, in the middle of the night, her father began to call his daughter, interrupting their millionth discussion about her departure.

"He remembers! He remembers me! You see! He's better." Olga leaped from the bed and ran to her father's room.

The old man welcomed her with a clear gentle look and in a language as alien as E.T.'s explained that he wanted to go to his mother's house. He said it just that way—"Mama's house"—and he held his arms out to his daughter as if he wanted to be picked up.

"Mama!" he cried and pressed against Olga's side with all his strength.

"I'm here," she managed to say. "All right, all right, I'll take you home."

Her father, without saying anything more, raised his eyes filled with tears. When he asked her for something to eat, Olga understood and she brought him all sorts of things, and he ate with the appetite of a boy who is in a hurry to grow strong to prepare for a grown-up adventure.

"Olga! Olga!" Ben grew impatient for his wife to return to bed. He asked himself what the devil those two were doing at that hour of the night, but out of laziness or a residue of modesty he didn't go to see. He was aware that there was some private matter between his wife and her father that was strictly their business.

"Olga!" he called. Then, since she wasn't coming back, he decided to get up. Instead of going in, he stayed by the door, spying on them in a way he never had before. Usually his motto was, "The less you know, the better." He had learned it when he was little; his father always said it when his mother started once again to tell about her suffering in czarist Russia before she reached America.

Through the crack in the half-open door, Ben saw his wife crouched on the floor next to her father with four photographs yellow with age set out like cards in front of her and an empty box of carved wood. His father-in-law was apparently sleeping with his big hands resting on his stomach over the padded coverlet.

"What are you doing?" asked Ben, entering.

"Do you want to kill me? You frightened me!" Olga groaned and went back to staring at the photographs she'd never seen before, trying to understand them. The more she looked, the more convinced she was that the middle-aged couple and the young married couple were the same people, her father's parents. The children dressed in sailor suits must be his brothers, or he as a child. She would never have believed, if someone had told her, that the man with a mustache dressed for his wedding was her own father with his first wife, and that the children in sailor suits were his murdered children. Eight-year-old David, the age of Jerry, and six-year-old Livia with the red hair ribbon in her blond hair full of ringlets, an angel come down to earth, killed before she could begin to live.

Even though Olga was convinced that she'd identified everyone in the photographs, with a voice full of anxiety, she asked her husband's opinion; she secretly hoped, without knowing exactly why, that Ben would say the same thing.

"Is it so important to know who they are?" Ben said, raising his voice, guessing that he was minimizing something.

"Yes," said Olga, holding her tears back with difficulty.

"Let me see . . ." He gave in, his voice annoyed, and took the photographs. After having glanced at them, he agreed that his wife was right, they must be her father's parents and his brothers. You could see how they resembled each other.

"They are my grandparents."

"Your uncles," Ben said with a smile, referring to the two children.

Instead of laughing with him, Olga burst out crying. Her small dark eyes shed black tears, desolate for all those unknown dead, relatives or nonrelatives, who were massacred in Europe. This she knew, yes, but nothing more. In her house it was forbidden to speak of it, as if it were something shameful, a dishonor for the victims as well.

As if the victims themselves had to deny the hatred and the massacres perpetrated against them.

Instead of comforting his wife, Ben said that crying this way was as absurd as her idea of taking her father to Hungary. He asked her how she could cry for unknown people who lived so long ago in that lousy rotten Europe.

"They weren't unknown," sobbed Olga, softly putting the photographs back in the box and replacing it between her father's hands cautiously and with respect, as if it were a relic.

She left the room and went back to her bed, followed by her husband, who continued to repeat that it was absurd to cry for people you didn't know.

"I'm not sure . . . ," confessed Olga after she had cried so much, she had no more tears.

"Is there an embassy or a Hungarian consulate here in America?" Ben thought out loud, his voice doubtful.

"There must be something, if people go to Hungary," murmured Olga. For Ben nothing existed unless he knew about it.

"I know a few more things than you do," he said resentfully, meaning his studies, the only thing he could boast about, like his parents who told everyone that he'd taken a law degree even if he ran the dry cleaner's, a trade not to be neglected, the source of a secure income.

"I'll call that Hungarian lady," said Olga, already sorry, and she said good night to him affectionately, just as she had for the ten years since they'd been married, from which time they'd slept together clutched tightly like two little orphans. She wouldn't have been able to sleep without her husband near her or without peace between them; she loved him a lot in her way and respected him both for his education and because he knew more than she did, tradition having destined her only for marriage and children. Her emancipation consisted only in shopping for clothes or makeup and having a car of her own like the other women of the neighborhood who knew how to drive. The car was as necessary as bread, even if it stayed in the garage—because most times they went to and from work together. If they went out, they went out together. They went to a birthday, a bar mitzvah, sometimes to the synagogue on important occasions like every respectable Jew from their privileged neighborhood of well-off immigrants. They all had shops and some property rented out in a poorer and uglier area, where the new immigrants coming from various countries, including Israel, lived. Many immigrants came from Russia through Israel, the jumping-off spot for those who wanted to get out and continue to places more economically promising.

Even though they'd been born in America, both Olga and Ben lived as their parents had, only they had more wealth. Ben had such respect for money that he hated to spend it except for necessities. While for Olga, love of money meant spending it as much as possible on food, cakes, dresses, scarves which she flaunted in her neighborhood because Manhattan was far away. And if you wanted to see the world, it was enough to turn on a television set so big that it filled an entire wall in the blue-carpeted living room.

Even Jerry was confined to the neighborhood, which had everything: schools, places for sports, rooms for ceremonies, a kind of cultural center where you could study Hebrew, get together on a holiday to bless Israel, learn modern and ancient Jewish songs. Though Israel was a real place, it lived in their hearts like a dream, a place to long for, where one would end up sooner or later, if not to live then to die there.

In Olga's family no one traveled abroad, America was everything for them. They didn't belong to one of those families scattered to the four corners of the globe. They were Americans and there was no need to cross the border when vacations could be taken in Miami, where many of them had small houses and met their neighbors. All things considered, this trip to Hungary was something so extraordinary in Olga's life that when she found herself asking for a visa in front of the Hungarian employee, she was confused and said that she and her father wanted to return to Hungary.

The Hungarian official looked at her with amazement. It was not going to be an easy matter, it would take time. And the man put a series of forms in front of Olga for her to fill with dates, names, explanations, reasons, etc. Olga, unaware of having been misunderstood, was immediately discouraged when faced by all these printed requests, which she couldn't answer.

"Oh no . . . I can't." She raised her eyes imploringly to the man.

"My father is ill," she tried to placate him. "We have to leave as soon as possible. Papa only speaks Hungarian. He wants to go home, you see? He no longer speaks English. It's the first time after forty years, can you let us go for at least a week? The doctor is sure it will do him good. Please help me." She was almost crying.

The man understood that it was a question of a tourist visa, and after a short while the matter was resolved. And the great day arrived.

Getting on an airplane for the first time at seventy-six, Alex seemed more like the husband than the father of his daughter. A couple on their honeymoon, so closely were they pressed to each other looking around, deeply moved and silent like two people waiting for their first night of love.

Alex was wearing a hat and his good suit from forty years before when he arrived in America; it was still new and fit him well, better than all his others. From the gray flannel of the well-tailored jacket emerged the overlarge collar of a blue shirt in the fashion of that epoch, with a gorgeous red tie that Olga loved. A blue cloth rain-coat and polished black shoes completed his look, partly American, partly European, the portrait of an immigrant without a specific look or origin.

Olga didn't want to go to the California Hotel. Maybe it would have been better to go to the Hilton, since there was a Hilton in Budapest where her father could have lived like a wealthy man—he who had once been poor, had suffered, and been forced to emigrate. But they advised her that the California Hotel was newer, with a view of the Danube, and at a better price.

She was dressed almost like a schoolgirl, with a red purse and shoes; she had the air of a grown child with that hair curled and blond as an angel's and her badly made-up face, which contrasted with her inspired gaze. She looked as satisfied as if she were taking her father to Lourdes or to the Promised Land, someplace where, thanks to her, a miracle would occur.

"Papa," she said, taking him by the arm while the airplane raced along the runway with deafening speed. "I'm taking you home, we're going to Hungary." She raised her voice to the man's ear. "What are you feeling, Papa? Can you tell me what you're feeling?"

Her father looked at her with an unmoving expression. Only his mouth had a slight quiver, the triumph of an accused innocent hearing words of absolution.

"Yes, yes," the old man said in Hungarian, meaning that everything was well.

"Will you teach me some Hungarian?" Olga asked when the airplane was already high in the air. "I have a dictionary here. Ah," she remembered, "you have to take this medicine," and she gave her father one of the many pills that he had to swallow daily. Thirteen to be exact.

"Please," read Olga in English, and she tried to read the same phrase in Hungarian but with such a bad accent that her father smiled and corrected her, immediately repeating the phrase several times before going on to other simple phrases.

Finally Olga wasn't feeling that reserve, that empty space in her father's heart that she was never able to fill as a child. And Alex, docile as a child in his mother's hands, seemed like a fragile object whom his daughter cared for as if he were Jerry. She covered him, made him eat, even fed him, but she didn't forget to question him about everything that he felt or remembered or thought, though she couldn't tell whether he understood where he was or where he was going.

Sometimes it seemed that her father was aware of everything, but at times phrases like "Let's go to school," "Let's go home," "Where are you taking me?" "Why are you taking me away?" would leave her discouraged. Thinking that now even this trip would be useless and that she had made a pointless sacrifice leaving her husband and child alone for the first time. Still, even in her moments of depression and self-pity she felt emotions she hadn't felt before, almost as if she herself and not her silent father, with his faraway eyes looking who knows where, were returning to her birthplace after forty years of absence. She even felt an unknown fear, an ancestral sorrow, as if her soul was tied to a black ribbon, attached in its deepest part. She counted the hours until their arrival, imagined not seeing but revisiting something dreamed about. She looked constantly at her watch, telling her father the time. Alex had never had a watch, he had never wanted one, as if for him time stopped when he lost his family. What had come afterward was like an appendix to a life already lived and finished. He himself was surprised to be alive. Because he was eating, working, walking, living, the only thing to do was to keep living until he died again without expecting too much from life, without being either happy or unhappy, simply existing because he had survived.

He had loved Olga with an anxious affection since she'd been little. Then he'd felt her to be so different from himself, felt at times as if he and his daughter were strangers, the more so because she wasn't allowed to know anything of his past, and the silence that his wife imposed on Alex about Auschwitz had ended by separating him from his daughter.

When the loudspeaker announced their imminent arrival, Olga's hands began to tremble as she adjusted her makeup, unable to draw a straight line on her swollen eyelids. Since she believed religiously in medicine, she had something for every possible symptom. She swallowed a tranquilizer, sighed trustingly, and went back to her makeup.

Unlike Olga, her father was as fresh-faced and bright-eyed as a child who has played hooky from school or won a trip as a prize.

"We've arrived, Papa, we're landing!" Olga stirred, staring through the small window at the ground, the landscape, that from high up seemed beautiful but still the same as any other place.

Her father's expression wavered between consciousness and unconsciousness, between sorrow and joy, between memory and oblivion. His memories emerged in brief flashes and disappeared behind a screen that was rent unexpectedly like a black curtain on a stage from which characters appear only for an instant and the audience is left to stare into the darkness, waiting for them to return.

Alex was grateful for every appearance of his family, whom he never saw dead but rather going about their daily life: his wife, Eva, was making their bed, the children were going to school, his mother was cooking, his tailor father was sewing with his broken thimble, the policemen strutted in the square—his friends turned their faces, and the priest said nothing when someone insulted a Jew. Alex didn't remember anything about the few years he had spent in Hungary after the war; it was as if they had never been.

When it was announced that in a few minutes the plane would land in Budapest's Ferihegy Airport, he felt faint, his heart and mind emptied, his ears and throat blocked, and he was so ill that Olga was afraid that he would die before they landed.

"Papa, Papa," she called to him. Frightened and needing help, she turned to the people sitting next to her. She had talked with them during the trip and knew they were going to the same hotel.

"Did you give him a sedative? He's experiencing some overwhelming emotion. Terrible. Terrible," they commented in chorus.

Olga gave him another tranquilizer and began to get him ready, she adjusted his tie, the collar of his shirt. She fixed his jacket, which had slipped down on his shoulders, put on his raincoat, and helped him get up, sustaining him and protecting him from the crowd that was trying to get off at the same time, pushing like starving people in line for food.

Exhausted but full of concern, Olga was afraid that her father would escape her. That he would disappear all of a sudden. While she held him up, she held tight to him like an anxious child who is going to her destruction but isn't afraid because she is with her father.

"This way please," said a flight attendant in English in a kind but firm voice, and there was no longer time for anyone to get emotional. Those few steps they took to the bus didn't even allow them to get the circulation going in their swollen and tingling legs, or to breathe freely in the open air. A second flight attendant herded them as a dog would a flock toward passport control, and the travelers complied, reassured and comforted that someone was looking after them.

Alex raised his eyes to the May sun and waved with one hand like someone who has seen a friend. Tears ran from his eyes without his being aware of them.

"Passport please," Olga heard in English when she got to the little window where a hand emerged from a uniform sleeve.

"You can speak Hungarian with my father," Olga said, pushing her father ahead of her.

"Don't worry," responded the young man in the booth without looking at the traveler. "Here we know some English. Welcome to Hungary!" he added, glancing at the photograph of the old man when he was young and then at Alex's present face. He stamped it and went on to the next person, the line pressed ahead, the attendant

pointed out a hostess who guided them to a gray room
with a low ceiling, where their baggage was already running along the automatic belt. A porter approached them,
volunteering in English, German, and Arabic.

The customs officials didn't look at anything and let
them go with a careless gesture, their expressions closed
and serious.

Outside, a boy in the uniform of the hotel held a sign with
California Hotel written on it. He was collecting clients one
by one. Repeating, "California Hotel," he guided them to a
bus on which the reassuring script stood out in gold letters.

The vividly painted bus for American tourists raced like
a toy between fields and small houses, bridges and dusty
roads, strips of dark asphalt and high buildings with dirty
walls and windows thrown open to the sun whose lace
curtains fluttered outside the glass, brushing the gerani-
ums in flower on the balconies.

As it happens in stories, after a turn, the bus arrived
in a park with a shining skyscraper, foursquare, a giant
cube of glass and cement that dominated the old city.

Having passed the automatic gate, Olga heard her
name, Mrs. Bernstein, and that of her father, Mr. Green,
surely a derivation of Grün.

"Yes," said Olga, going ahead with her father among a
group of Arabs annoyed at their slow progress toward the
man who was calling to them from behind a counter.

"Mrs. Bernstein and Mr. Green?" asked the man hurriedly. "Your passports please," he added, without waiting for a response, and he had scarcely received them when he gave them the key to their room on the thirteenth floor.

"They're taking our passports." A lady was alarmed.

"I thought there'd be a lot of Russians, instead it's full of Arabs," whispered a second lady to her husband.

"I heard German," someone had the time to say, and already they were in front of one of the four glass elevators, which could be seen running along the internal walls of the skyscraper through flowering terraces between the floors that formed a single mass of color and greenery. Alex rose in a heaven of flowers and looked at the ground far below and full of trees.

When the glass cage stopped abruptly at the thirteenth floor, Olga, who was slightly dizzy, no longer knew which way to go, she didn't understand she was in an internal corridor with red carpeting and a string of doors enameled with a brilliant military green.

Alex, completely lost, had to be pushed along into the fashionably furnished room complete with refrigerator, television, and radio.

Olga, incredulous, opened the refrigerator and turned on the radio, which released the familiar voice of Sinatra. She pressed the button of the television and saw the images of an old film with Elizabeth Taylor, who was speaking Hungarian.

It seemed so funny that she burst into relieved laughter that was close to tears.

"Papa, Papa, do you hear? She's speaking Hungarian! Finally someone is speaking Hungarian!"

Her father looked at her, serious, disoriented. He hadn't the slightest idea what his daughter was talking about.

"Liz," repeated Olga, shutting off the TV. "Liz." Smiling, she named all her screen favorites: Liz, Marlon, Al, Jane. Jerry and Ben would have known exactly who she was talking about.

For a moment she felt very alone, so alone and far from her family and her America that she felt she might die, or that she'd never be able to return.

"I'll call. I'll call Jerry and Ben." She grabbed the phone, leaving her father standing in the middle of the room.

The telephone operator rapidly connected her with New York. Jerry and Ben, who always slept together when she wasn't there, were awakened in the middle of the night. Olga told them about her long trip, the fantastic hotel for a hundred dollars a night, and a Hungary that no longer seemed like Hungary.

"Today we're not going anywhere. We'll eat in the room. We'll rest," she said, turning to her father after she had finished the long telephone conversation. Only then did she notice that her father was standing with his raincoat on and his hat on his head.

"We're here, Papa, take your hat off, sit down." She pushed him to one of the armchairs with a footrest.

"Should I read you what's on the menu? Do you want goulash? *Csirke paprikàs? Polacsinta?*" She laughed, reading the menu in Hungarian. "Let's have a little of everything. We ought to celebrate our arrival! Let's order everything."

Her father nodded consent. He smiled. He took off his raincoat by himself and looked around like someone who is trying to understand where he is.

A waiter knocked at the door. He entered, pushing a cart loaded with food, shining glasses, luxurious tableware, porcelain plates. Like a film.

"My God," exclaimed Olga, clasping her hands in wonder.

"Can I offer you anything else?" asked the waiter in the English of a good student who has just learned the language and is trying hard to use it.

Everyone speaks English except my father, thought Olga, and it made her laugh.

English was becoming a universal language, and her father had forgotten it or was refusing to speak it. Maybe to punish her? Because she had married Ben, whom her father had never liked.

"What's your name?" Olga asked the waiter.

"Sandor," said the boy. "Alexander," he gave the international version of his name. "Alex," he abbreviated it, looking into his interlocutor's face as if surprised.

"Sandor?" Olga said finally with a perfect Hungarian accent. "That's my father's name too, isn't that right, Papa? Say your name in Hungarian," she urged him.

"Sandor . . . Sandor," said the old man as if to himself, shaking his head to say that yes, there was a Sandor. Then repeating a third time his forgotten name, he raised his eyes to the waiter who had the same name, and there the waiter was, quietly waiting for their orders.

"Why don't you speak to my father a little in Hungarian," Olga gave him a seductive smile while she searched in her purse for a dollar to tip him.

"What would you like?" The waiter, who hadn't understood the request of the agitated American, finally opened his mouth.

"My father," Olga explained more slowly, "he's been away from his country for forty years but he speaks Hungarian well. In fact he only speaks Hungarian! Maybe if he speaks his language, he'll be cured. Ask him something. How he is? If he has had a good trip, I don't know . . . talk to him," Olga said, growing impatient.

The waiter still didn't understand what was being asked of him, though he guessed that the old man was originally Hungarian and that he spoke Hungarian. But because he wanted to be sure and also because he was very good at pronouncing easy phrases like, "Do you speak Hungarian?," he addressed him in English.

To prove that he could speak Hungarian, the only thing that came to the old man's mind was the children's song that he had played at Jerry's birthday party.

"Little spotted calf without ears or tail, ta ta ta ta ta and so full of spots. Why are you taking me to Pest?"

In the great inner courtyard someone heard the song and, leaning over a flowering terrace, joined his voice to the voices of Olga and Alex who were singing together, eating, and giving toasts. Olga seemed like a child overwhelmed by the freedom to do whatever she wished, drink a little, eat a lot, and sing at the top of her lungs with her father.

Alex, free of his memory and his years, unaware of where he was, felt a weightless happiness. He imagined that instead of beating the rhythm on the arm of a chair, he was beating it on the piano where once, in another life, he knew how to play.

Olga had never seen her father this way, and such happiness, like her parent's unknown past, only frightened her.

"Papa!" She stopped singing, looked at him, and understood that this man, happy as she had never seen him before, was her father in a world of his own from which he would never return.

She felt a gentle sorrow for that man without memory but alive, still alive, younger even, more childlike, a child. She thought that it was no longer necessary to stay in Hungary for a whole week, she could take him home now. For someone without a memory, it is unimportant where he lives.

There is nothing more to read. I am left empty, disappointed. I notice that the pages, which I've thrown on the floor as soon as I read them, have been torn to pieces by the nails and teeth of my cats, who, like me, have a passion for paper.

Instead of reproaching them, I smile and hurry to unpack my suitcase, to put everything in its place as though I'd never left. Although I know I've made that trip, I don't want to see any trace of it, or measure it against real time. It already seems to me that I was in a faraway, internal place about which I can no longer speak or write.

In the box of linen, I find myself face-to-face with the gun. It no longer frightens me, but I don't want to touch it, only to get rid of it at once. I bring my purse close and, without touching it, wrap the weapon in the soft leather. With confident steps I head for the exit. From habit I stop at the bathroom door and enter automatically for a glance in the mirror. I rest the purse on the toilet seat. If the gun could pass through, I would throw it in.

I look at myself and see my usual fall pallor, my tan already gone. I need a little rouge. The only rouge I have is in my purse. Cautiously I slip my hand inside. I feel my house keys, pens, tobacco on the bottom, the cold of the weapon, and a haphazard array of other things. My purse is a disorganized warehouse, like my memory, where I can't find what I need when I need it, like the death of my father at Dachau. I make an involuntary, quick gesture, angry, I shake the purse, disturb the pistol, the gun goes off. Have I been fired at, or have I fired at myself? I look at my face becoming twisted in the mirror as the glass flies into a million pieces, destroying my image that seems like an exploded star, a crystal six-pointed star with a black hole in its forehead. But there is no blood. Only the mirror has been hit. It's incredible! Beautiful!

The only thing that comes to my mind is the children's song that I made old Alex sing in my torn story. I too begin to sing it while in an unbroken corner of the mirror I see with amazement my image intact, made young again.

In my youthful smile I read a kind of complicity, like someone who has escaped danger for the millionth time through a secret mysterious pact with the unnameable, someone without image or form, my eternal and invisible playmate.

Modern Language Association of America
Texts and Translations

To purchase MLA publications,
visit www.mla.org/bookstore

Texts

Anna Banti. *"La signorina" e altri racconti.* Ed. and introd. Carol Lazzaro-Weis. 2001.

Bekenntnisse einer Giftmischerin, von ihr selbst geschrieben. Ed. and introd. Raleigh Whitinger and Diana Spokiene. 2009.

Adolphe Belot. *Mademoiselle Giraud, ma femme.* Ed and introd. Christopher Rivers. 2002.

Dovid Bergelson. אָפּגאַנג. Ed. and introd. Joseph Sherman. 1999.

Elsa Bernstein. *Dämmerung: Schauspiel in fünf Akten.* Ed. and introd. Susanne Kord. 2003.

Edith Bruck. *Lettera alla madre.* Ed. and introd. Gabriella Romani. 2006.

Mikhail Bulgakov. Дон Кихот. Introd. Margarita Marinova and Scott Pollard. 2014.

Isabelle de Charrière. *Lettres de Mistriss Henley publiées par son amie.* Ed. Joan Hinde Stewart and Philip Stewart. 1993.

Isabelle de Charrière. *Trois femmes: Nouvelle de l'Abbé de la Tour.* Ed. and introd. Emma Rooksby. 2007.

François-Timoléon de Choisy, Marie-Jeanne L'Héritier, and Charles Perrault. *Histoire de la Marquise-Marquis de Banneville.* Ed. Joan DeJean. 2004.

Sophie Cottin. *Claire d'Albe.* Ed. and introd. Margaret Cohen. 2002.

Marceline Desbordes-Valmore. *Sarah.* Ed. Deborah Jenson and Doris Y. Kaddish. 2008.

Claire de Duras. *Ourika.* Ed. Joan DeJean. Introd. DeJean and Margaret Waller. 1994.

Şeyh Galip. *Hüsn ü Aşk.* Ed. and introd. Victoria Rowe Holbrook. 2005.

Françoise de Graffigny. *Lettres d'une Péruvienne.* Introd. Joan DeJean and Nancy K. Miller. 1993.

Sofya Kovalevskaya. Нигилистка. Ed. and introd. Natasha Kolchevska. 2001.

Thérèse Kuoh-Moukoury. *Rencontres essentielles.* Introd. Cheryl Toman. 2002.

Juan José Millás. *"Trastornos de carácter" y otros cuentos.* Introd. Pepa Anastasio. 2007.

Emilia Pardo Bazán. *"El encaje roto" y otros cuentos.* Ed. and introd. Joyce Tolliver. 1996.

Rachilde. *Monsieur Vénus: Roman matérialiste.* Ed. and introd. Melanie Hawthorne and Liz Constable. 2004.

Marie Riccoboni. *Histoire d'Ernestine.* Ed. Joan Hinde Stewart and Philip Stewart. 1998.

George Sand. *Gabriel.* Ed. Kathleen Robin Hart. 2010.

Eleonore Thon. *Adelheit von Rastenberg.* Ed. and introd. Karin A. Wurst. 1996.

Translations

Anna Banti. *"The Signorina" and Other Stories.* Trans. Martha King and Carol Lazzaro-Weis. 2001.

Adolphe Belot. *Mademoiselle Giraud, My Wife.* Trans. Christopher Rivers. 2002.

Dovid Bergelson. *Descent.* Trans. Joseph Sherman. 1999.

Elsa Bernstein. *Twilight: A Drama in Five Acts.* Trans. Susanne Kord. 2003.

Edith Bruck. *Letter to My Mother.* Trans. Brenda Webster with Gabriella Romani. 2006.

Mikhail Bulgakov. *Don Quixote.* Trans. Margarita Marinova. 2014.

Isabelle de Charrière. *Letters of Mistress Henley Published by Her Friend.* Trans. Philip Stewart and Jean Vaché. 1993.

Isabelle de Charrière. *Three Women: A Novel by the Abbé de la Tour.* Trans. Emma Rooksby. 2007.

François-Timoléon de Choisy, Marie-Jeanne L'Héritier, and Charles Perrault. *The Story of the Marquise-Marquis de Banneville.* Trans. Steven Rendall. 2004.

Confessions of a Poisoner, Written by Herself. Trans. Raleigh Witinger and Diane Spokiene. 2009.

Sophie Cottin. *Claire d'Albe.* Trans. Margaret Cohen. 2002.

Marceline Desbordes-Valmore. *Sarah.* Trans. Deborah Jenson and Doris Y. Kaddish. 2008.

Claire de Duras. *Ourika.* Trans. John Fowles. 1994.

Şeyh Galip. *Beauty and Love.* Trans. Victoria Rowe Holbrook. 2005.

Françoise de Graffigny. *Letters from a Peruvian Woman.* Trans. David Kornacker. 1993.

Sofya Kovalevskaya. *Nihilist Girl.* Trans. Natasha Kolchevska with Mary Zirin. 2001.

Thérèse Kuoh-Moukoury. *Essential Encounters*. Trans. Cheryl Toman. 2002.

Juan José Millás. *"Personality Disorders" and Other Stories*. Trans. Gregory B. Kaplan. 2007.

Emilia Pardo Bazán. *"Torn Lace" and Other Stories*. Trans. María Cristina Urruela. 1996.

Rachilde. *Monsieur Vénus: A Materialist Novel*. Trans. Melanie Hawthorne. 2004.

Marie Riccoboni. *The Story of Ernestine*. Trans. Joan Hinde Stewart and Philip Stewart. 1998.

George Sand. *Gabriel*. Trans. Kathleen Robin Hart and Paul Fenouillet. 2010.

Eleonore Thon. *Adelheit von Rastenberg*. Trans. George F. Peters. 1996.

Texts and Translations in One Volume Anthologies

Modern Italian Poetry. Ed. and trans. Ned Condini. Introd. Dana Renga. 2009

Modern Urdu Poetry. Ed., introd., and trans. M. A. R. Habib. 2003.

Nineteenth-Century Women's Poetry from France. Ed. Gretchen Schultz. Trans. Anne Atik, Michael Bishop, Mary Ann Caws, Melanie Hawthorne, Rosemary Lloyd, J. S. A. Lowe, Laurence Porter, Christopher Rivers, Schultz, Patricia Terry, and Rosanna Warren. 2008.

Nineteenth-Century Women's Poetry from France. Ed. Anna-Marie Aldaz. Introd. Susan Kirkpatrick. Trans. Aldaz and W. Robert Walker. 2008.

Spanish American Modernismo. Ed. Kelly Washbourne. Trans. Washbourne with Sergio Waisman. 2007.